THE AUTUMN LAND

I stopped about six feet from the creature and he didn't look as bad close up as he did at a distance. His eyes seemed to be kind and gentle and his funny face, alien as it was, had a sort of peacefulness about it. But even so, you can't always tell with aliens.

We stood there looking at one another. The both of us understood there was no use of talking. We just stood and sized one another up.

Then the creature took a couple of steps and reached out a hand that was more like a claw than a hand. He took my hand in his and tugged for me to come.

There were just two things to do – either snatch my hand away or go.

I went.

Clifford D. Simak

The AUTUMN LAND
and other stories

*Collected and edited
by Francis Lyall*

Mandarin

A Mandarin Paperback

THE AUTUMN LAND

First published 1990
by Mandarin Paperbacks
Michelin House, 81 Fulham Road, London SW3 6RB

Mandarin is an imprint of the Octopus Publishing Company

ISBN 0 7493 0185 6
A CIP catalogue record for this title
is available from the British Library

**Printed in Great Britain
by Cox & Wyman Ltd, Reading**

Contents

INTRODUCTION

Some writers hew their work from close to the wellsprings of humanity, touching on deep things which resonate within the psyche, and thereby stamping their work with an outstanding individuality. Clifford D. Simak is one of these distinctive voices. I recall coming across his stories – it was *City* (1951) – early in my acquaintanceship with science fiction, and I still remember the impact it made. This was far from the facile transplanted Westerns that I had so often encountered. After that experience Simak was an author to be searched for, and every new story devoured. It was therefore a great joy to meet CDS years later in Minneapolis in autumn 1981, and marvellous to me that our friendship continued and ripened, closing only with his death in April 1988. It has also been a privilege to be permitted to collect some of his fiction and make it available in book form to a fresh generation of sf readers. This is the fourth such collection. Cliff had seen and approved an earlier version of the introduction to these stories, but more must now be said, which his innate modesty might not have permitted.

Talent is something to be prized in all forms of art and entertainment. Early this year I was in company. The radio was playing unfamiliar music which we tried to identify. The best we could agree was that Hindemith was one possibility and Walton another. We even swapped over in our opinions as the music played on. The piece turned out to be Walton's 'Variations on a Theme by Hindemith'. Two characteristic musical voices showed in the piece, but the combination misled us as one or other element predominated. Hindemith or Walton can be readily recognised; put them together and it was difficult to name the composer. But it is the element of the identifiable voice that I would take from that story.

It can be the same in science fiction. Among the rafts of semi-successful clones, there are unmistakable writers. Indeed, the best writers in all forms of literature have each an individuality which is a major part of their attraction. Regrettably (and despite the blurb on the cover of virtually every new book), one rarely comes upon a truly distinctive voice among the torrent of words that make up today's science fiction. (Fantasy is worse.) There are exceptions, of course. One would not wish to denigrate such as Le Guin, Triptree or McCaffery. And it may be that things have not changed over the years, for there are many names in the 'pulps' which have deservedly not survived. But it is significant that the senior authors of the genre – those whose work has lasted – are all clear and unmistakable individuals. Pick up a story by Clarke, Asimov, Heinlein, Clement, Pohl or Simak and even if you have previously read only a little of the author you will recognise that author's particular voice. Just as music is a matter of theme, intonation, tempo and orchestration, so the author's chosen themes, style, pace, plot, setting, and his 'science' render the voice identifiable, and a reader is or is not attracted. The name is a hall-mark, an assurance of a particular blend of qualities.

Over more than fifty-five years, my friend Clifford D. Simak, though a part-time author and busy at his newspaper work, published more than two hundred short stories and twenty-seven novels. Many full-time writers have had less success. Nor is publication alone the mark of his achievement. He was regularly nominated for sf awards. When I visited his home in Minnetonka outside Minneapolis, the mantelpiece in his study supported three Hugos (for 'The Big Front Yard', 1959; *Way Station*, 1964; and 'The Grotto of the Dancing Deer', 1980), and that most beautiful of the awards, a Nebula (for 'The Grotto of the Dancing Deer', 1980 – which also won the Locus short story award for that year). Further, in 1977 he had received the Nebula Grand Master award of the Science Fiction Writers of America as well as the Jupiter Award (for *A Heritage of Stars*), and in 1953 he was awarded the International Fantasy Award for *City*.

As a sf writer CDS was innovative, contributing much to the portfolio of notions which are the staple of the genre. That sf is a literature of ideas is a truism, but more sf notions can be traced to CDS than a strict proportion of his wordage among the bulkiness of sf suggests. Again, his questioning approach often sheds a new light on or shows a new side to notions accepted in sf, in other literature and in society. Within the field he is particularly celebrated for his reverence for traditional mores, for the deep caring which surfaces again and again in his work, and for the frequent pastoral settings in which the stories are located. These characteristics developed early. Although his first stories conformed to the prevalent ethos of the 1930s one can see even in them the seeds that later were to flower so abundantly.

CDS began his sf career in 1931–2 with a burst of five stories (four in *Wonder Stories*) but then decided that he did not like the way that the sf magazines were developing. Uncertain that he wanted even to try to satisfy the then editors, he thought he would not write more in the genre. He therefore reconciled himself to leaving the sf scene, although in 1934 he did write a further remarkable story, 'The Creator' (recently republished in I. Asimov, G. Sebrowski and M. H. Greenberg, eds., *Creations: The Quest for Origins in Story and Science*, 1984). This was written at the request of W. L. Crawford for his semi-professional magazine *Marvel Tales*, and is notable for its treatment of God, elliptically questioning both creation and God's character in a way novel for its time, and in a manner which would not have been acceptable in the normal 'pulps' of the day.

'The Creator' was considered by its author to be his final sf story. However, the appointment of John W. Campbell as editor of *Astounding SF* in 1937 recalled him to the field. CDS felt that he could work with Campbell. 'Rule 18', the first story in this collection, was the first of many which Campbell published. I include it for three reasons. First it is here on merit. Second, it is here because it was an historic re-entry of a major author into science fiction. Third, it is here for the curious, those who are interested in sf history. The young Isaac Asimov hated 'Rule 18' and said so in the *ASF* letters column. In several places (most recently in his obituary note for Cliff in *Locus*,

9

Issue No. 329, vol. 21, No. 6, June 1988) Asimov has told how surprised he was to get a response from the author – a letter from CDS asking for more details of the criticism so that he could learn how to avoid the perceived defects in his future writing. Asimov re-read the story, changed his mind, and so began a lasting friendship between the two. What had upset the Good Doctor was CDS's method of telling the story in separate scenes without the transitional material customary at the time. The effect is to move the story along, gaining in pace. Asimov himself adopted the device, which is now so common as to be unremarkable. Indeed, its absence is now a ground of criticism. Having read CDS, and liked his style, Asimov also sought to follow him in the simplicity and clarity of his writing and his naturalism in dialogue. We have seen the result. 'Rule 18' is therefore a pivotal story in the development of modern sf writing – though presumably in an alternate universe there are many other causes of the Asimov phenomenon!

'Rule 18' is typical Simak. Granted that the base is flawed, for we have now seen what Mars is like, nonetheless the story is still fun and in its dealing both with time and the trickery of rules shows elements that CDS was to go on to explore elsewhere. Indeed it is not too much to say that CDS was fascinated by questions of time and time paradox, many of his stories dealing with these matters) compare with the tales in *The Marathon Photograph*, 1986, and the novel *Time and Again*, 1951). 'Gleaners', later in these pages, is a further, equally lighthearted look at questions of time.

'Gleaners' also shows another side of CDS. There is a quiet dignity as well as a lot of humour about the story. Hallock Spencer remains true to the basic principles of honesty and decency, and reaps a rich harvest. That is a frequent message of the Simak story. One cannot aim at gain through sticking by traditional values, but, where traditional values are observed for their own sake, they may be accompanied by other attractive consequences. That is true to life. 'Contraption', where innocent friendliness has more than its own reward, is another variation on this theme.

Such stories can be traced to CDS's upbringing. He was reared in the farm country on the bluffs that lie south of the Wisconsin river in the few miles before it reaches the mighty Mississippi. There he drank deep of traditional rural values.

There he learned that *what* a man is is more important than *who* he is. That can work out in different ways. In 'Jackpot' it may be that to travel is better than to arrive; that the urge ever to seek is a fundamental part of Man. Being true to oneself may require that one does not take every benefit that may be available. But 'Courtesy', the other 'off-planet' story in this collection, returns to the other pole. There we see CDS's great respect for sentience, underscored by the apparent result when there is no respect of another who may appear alien. The story was published in 1951 – long before segregation had been done away with. I wonder how many it influenced. My one cavil with it is in the naming. The names repeat those of another exploration team in the CDS *oeuvre*, and I regret that.

Last, and as title story, there is 'The Autumn Land'. The internal evidence of this story, and having driven around the area, allows me to assert that this story is located in the terrain of CDS's youth. Nelson Rand, driving east from California to Chicago in the hopes of a job, sees, somehow, the future devastation of Dubuque, and escapes from there back to his own 'valley of the magic moment' of his childhood. There he finds the village, the old lady, the old man, the sounds of the children playing in the dusk, and the Milkman.

'The Autumn Land' is one of the supreme examples of CDS's art. The writing is spare and yet like a master organist CDS touches many keys and runs the range of the organ stops. The ideas are mind-stretching, the effect solemnising. Where is the village? What happened to the city, and the photographs? Who or what is the Milkman? Where does the old man go? What is beyond the wilderness of grass? What is the village? Would Rand like a gun, a cross, some symbol, a volume of philosophy, or perhaps some currency? 'I merely mention certain things upon which humans place reliance . . .' There is a disinterested, almost puzzled, care there, which echoes deep. And then: 'There'll be others coming. There's always others coming.' We leave Rand waiting for those others. Truth is here, not articulated but certainly to be grasped. It is true to the life of a writer: it is true to the life of each of us if we think about it. It touches that note which so many of CDS's stories sound, a note of awe and mystery which only the best sf sounds. I grieve that the mind that produced this pearl will produce no more.

Science fiction is a complete literature. Tragedy to comedy, grand opera to children's ditties are all encompassed within it. These stories by my friend are contributions drawn from across a rich writing career. Enjoy them. That was his principal aim.

Aberdeen, Scotland.   F. Lyall
February, 1990.

RULE 18

Rule XVIII – Each player on the respective teams must be able to present documentary evidence that he is of pure blood of the planet upon whose team he plays for an unbroken span of at least ten generations. Verification of the aforesaid documentary evidence and approval of the players upon this point shall be the duty of the Interplanetary Athletic Control Board – From the eligibility section of the Official Rule Book for the Annual Terrestrial-Martian Football Game.

Year 2479

I

The mighty bowl resounded to the throaty war cry of the Druzecs, ancient tribe of the Martian Drylands. The cry seemed to blast the very dome of the sky. The purple and red of the Martian stands heaved tumultuously as the Martian visitors waved their arms and screamed their victory. The score was 19–0. For the sixty-seventh consecutive year the Martians had defeated the Earth team. And for the forty-second consecutive year the Terrestrial team had failed to score even a single point.

There had been a time when an Earth eleven occasionally did defeat the Red Warriors. But that had been years ago. It was something that oldsters, mumbling in their beards, told about as if it were a legendary tale from the ancient past. Evil days had fallen upon the Gold and Green squads.

And again this year the pick of the entire Earth, the Terrestrial crack football machine, had been trampled underfoot by the smashing forward wall of Martians, slashed to bits by the ferocious attack of the Red Planet backfield.

Not that the Earth had not tried. Every team member had fought a heart-rending game, had put forth every ounce of strength, every shred of football sense, every last trickle of stout courage. Not that the Earth team was not good. It was good. It was the pick of the entire world, an All-Terrestrial eleven, selected on its merits of the preceding year and trained for an entire year under the mentorship of August Snelling, one of the canniest coaches the game had ever known. It was neither of these. It was just that the Martian team was better.

Bands blared. The two teams were trailed off the field. The Martian victory cry continued to rend the skies, rolling in wave after successive wave from leathern throats.

The Earth stands were emptied quietly, but the Martians remained, trumpeting their prowess. When the Martians did leave the amphitheatre, they took over the city of New York after the manner of football crowds since time immemorial. They paraded their mascot, the grotesque, ten-legged *zimpa*, through the streets. Some of them got drunk on Martian *bocca*, a potent liquor banned by law from sale on Earth, but always available in hundreds of speakeasies throughout the city. There were a few clashes between Martian and Earth delegations and some of the Martians were jailed. New York would be a bedlam until the Martian Special, huge space liner chartered for the game, roared out of its cradle at midnight for the return run to Mars.

In the editorial rooms of the *Evening Rocket* Hap Folsworth, sports-writer extraordinary, explained it in a blur of submerged rage and admitted futility.

'They just don't grow them big enough or strong enough on Earth anymore,' he declared. 'We are living too damn easy. We're getting soft. Each generation is just a bit softer than the last. There's no more hard work to be done. Machines do things for us. Machines mine ores, raise crops, manufacture everything from rocket ships to safety pins. All we got to do is push levers and punch buttons. A hell of a lot of muscle you can develop punching a button.

'Where did they get the famous players of the past? Of a couple, three hundred years ago, or of a thousand years ago, if you like?' Hap blared. 'I'll tell you where they got them! They got them out of mines and lumber camps and off the farms — places where you had to have guts and brawn to make a living.

'But we got smart. We fixed it so nobody has to work anymore. There are husky Earth lads, lots of them — in Martian mining camps and in Venus lumber camps and out on the Ganymede engineering projects. But every damn one of them has got Martian or Venusian blood in his veins. And Rule Eighteen says you got to be lily-pure for ten generations. If you ask me, that's a hell of a rule.'

Hap looked around to see how his audience was taking his talk. All of them seemed to be in agreement and he went on. What he was saying wasn't new. It had been said thousands of times by thousands of sports-writers in thousands of different ways, but Hap recited it after each game. He enjoyed doing it. He chewed off the end of a Venus-weed cigar and went on.

'The Martians aren't soft. Their planet is too old and exhausted and nature-ornery for them to be soft. They got brawn and guts and their coaches somehow manage to pound some football sense into their thick heads. Why, football is just their meat — even if we did teach them the game.'

He lit his cigar and puffed contentedly.

'Say,' he asked as the others stood in respectful silence, 'has anyone seen Russell today?'

They shook their heads.

The sports-writer considered the answer and then said, without emotion, 'When he does show up, I'm going to boot him right smack-dab into the stratosphere. I sent him out two days ago to get an interview with Coach Snelling and he hasn't showed up yet.'

'He'll probably be around next week,' suggested a copy-boy. 'He's probably just sleeping one off somewhere.'

'Sure, I know,' mourned Hap, 'and when he does come in, he'll drag in a story so big the chief will kiss him for remembering us.'

Coach August Snelling delivered his annual after-the-Martian-game oration to his team.

'When you went out on the field today,' he told them, 'I

15

praised you and pleaded with you to get out there and do some of the things I taught you to do. And what did you do? You went out there and you laid down on me. You laid down on the Earth. You laid down on five hundred thousand people in the stands who paid good hard cash to see a football game. You let those big dumb-bells push you all over the lot. You had a dozen good plays, every one of them good for ground. And did you use them? You did not!

'You're a bunch of lollipops. A good punch in the ribs and you roll over and bark. Maybe there'll be some of you on the team next year and maybe there won't. But if there are, I want you to remember that when we go up to Mars I intend to bring back that trophy if I have to steal it. And if I don't, I'll stop the ship midway and dump you all out. And then jump out myself.'

But this didn't mean much. For Coach Snelling, ace of the Earth coaches, had said the same thing, in substance, to Earth teams after each Martian game for the last twenty years.

Tantalizing shadows, queer, alien shadows flitted in the ground glass of the outré machine. Alexis Androvitch held his breath and watched. The shadows took form, then faded, but they had held tangible shape long enough for Alexis to glimpse what he wished to see, a glimpse that filled him with a supreme sense of triumph.

The first step was completed. The second would be harder, but now that the first was accomplished – now that he really had some proof of his theories – progress would be faster.

Alexis snapped off the machine and stepped to a bowl. There he washed his hands. Shrugging into a coat, he opened the door and trudged up the steps to the street above.

On the avenue he was greeted by the raucous cries of the auto-newsstands, 'Earth loses 19–0 . . . Read all about it . . . Extra . . . Extra . . .' repeating over and over the words recorded on the sound film within them.

Customers placed coins in the slot, shoved a lever, and out came a paper with huge purple headlines and natural-colour photo reproductions of the game.

The vari-coloured neon street lamps flicked on. Smoothly operating street machines slid swiftly down the broad, glassy pavement. Overhead purred the air-lane traffic.

From somewhere came the muffled sound of the Drylands war cry as the Martians continued their celebration of victory.

Alexis Androvitch walked on, unmindful of the war cries, of the blaring newsstands. He was not interested in athletics. He was on his way to a garden to enjoy a glass of beer and a plate of cheese.

Rush Culver, Wisconsin '45, was struggling with calculus. Exams stared him in the face and Rush freely admitted that he was a fool for having chosen maths instead of zoology. Somehow or other he wasn't so bright at figures.

It was late. The other fellows in the house were asleep hours ago. A white moon painted the windows of the house opposite in delicate silver squares and rectangles. A night wind sighed softly in the elms outside. A car raced up State Street and the old clock in the music hall tower tolled out the hour with steady beat of bell.

Rush mopped his brow and dug deeper into his book.

He failed to hear the door of his room open softly and close again. He did not turn about until he heard the scuff of feet on the floor.

A tall stranger stood in the room.

Rush looked at him with something of disgust. He was dressed in purple shorts and a semi-metallic shirt that flashed and glinted in the soft rays of the desk lamp. His feet were shod in sandals. His head was verging on the bald and his face was pale, almost as if he had resorted to face powder.

'Just home from a masquerade?' asked Rush.

The stranger did not answer at once, but stood silently, looking at the student.

When he did speak, his voice was soft and slurred and his English carried an accent Rush could not place.

'You will pardon the intrusion,' the stranger said. 'I did not wish to disturb you. I merely wanted to know if you are Rush Culver, fullback for the Wisconsin football team.'

'I have a good mind to lay one on you,' said Rush with feeling. 'Almost three o'clock in the morning and me wrestling with maths. Want to know if I'm Rush Culver. Want my autograph, maybe?'

The stranger smiled. 'I hardly understand,' he said. 'I know

17

nothing of autographs. But you are having trouble. Maybe I can help.'

'If you can, brother,' declared Rush, 'I'll lend you some clothes so you can get home without being pinched. The cops in this town are tough on students.'

The stranger walked forward, picked up the book, glanced at it and threw it aside. 'Simple,' he said. 'Elementary. This problem.'

He bent over and ran a finger down the work sheet. His words came softly, in measured cadence.

'It is this way . . . and this way . . . and this way . . .'

Rush stared. 'Say, it's simple,' he chortled. 'But it never was explained to me that way before. I can see how it goes now.'

He rose from the chair and confronted the stranger.

'Who are you?' he asked.

II

Hap Folsworth snarled through his cigar at Jimmy Russell.

'So you came back empty-handed,' he growled. 'You, the demon reporter for the *Evening Rocket*. In the name of double-dipped damnation, can't you ever do anything? I send you out on a simple errand. "Just run over to Coach Snelling," says I, "and get the line-up on the Earth team". Any office boy could do that. And you come back without it. All you had to do was ask the coach for it and he would hand it to you.'

Jimmy snarled back. 'Why, you space-locoed tramp,' he roared, 'if it's as simple as that, go down and get it yourself. If you ever lifted yourself out of that easy chair and found out what was happening, instead of sitting there thinking up wisecracks, you might call yourself a newspaperman. I could have told you a week ago there was something screwy about this Earth team. All sorts of rumours floating around. How much news have we printed about it? How much has *Morning Space-Ways* and the *Evening Star* printed about it? But you sit here and look wise and tell the world that Snelling is just using some high-powered psychology to get the Martians' goat. Making it appear he has some new material or some new plays. Say, that old buzzard hasn't had a new play since the first spaceship blew up.'

Hap snorted and rescued the cigar. He jabbed a vicious forefinger at the reporter.

'Listen,' he yelled. 'I was a newsman when you were still in diapers. I'll lay you five to one I can call up Snelling and have him agree to give us a list of players.'

Silently Jimmy picked up the visaphone set and handed it to Hap.

The sports-writer set the dial for the field-house wave length. A face appeared in the glass.

'Let me speak to the coach,' said Hap.

The glass went dead as the connection was shifted.

The face of Coach Snelling appeared.

'Say, coach . . .' said Hap. But that was as far as he got.

'Listen, Hap,' said the coach, 'I'm a friend of yours. I like you. You've said some nice things about me when the wolves were out after my hide. If I had anything to tell anyone, I'd tell it to the *Evening Rocket*. But I haven't anything to tell anyone. I want you fellows to understand that. And if you send any more of those high-powered reporters of yours around I'll just naturally kick them out on their faces. That's a promise.'

The phone went dead.

Jimmy laughed at the bewildered stare in Hap's eyes.

'Pay up,' he demanded.

The coach's office was empty and Jimmy was glad of that. It fitted in with his plans.

He hadn't liked the nasty light in the chief's eyes when he had been told to get a list of the Earth's new team. Nothing about *how* he was to get it. No suggestions at all, although it was understood that it couldn't be gotten directly from the coach. Presumably some other means of obtaining it would have to be worked out.

But while the chief had said nothing about how to get it, he had said plenty about what would happen if he returned without it. That was the way with editors, Jimmy reflected glumly. No gratitude. Just a hunk of ice for a heart. Who was it had given the *Rocket* a scoop on the huge gambling syndicate which had tried to buy a victory for the Earth team? Who was it had broken the yarn about the famous jewel-ship robbery off the orbit of Callisto when a governmental clique – which later went to the Moon penal colony – had moved Heaven and

Earth to suppress the story? Who had phoned the first flash and later written an eye-witness story that boosted circulation over 6,000 copies concerning the gang murder of Danny Carsten? No one other than James Russell, reporter for the *Evening Rocket*. And yet, here he was, chasing a team list with sulphurous threats hanging over his head if he failed.

Jimmy tiptoed into the coach's office. He wasn't used to getting his news this way and it made him nervous.

There were papers on the desk. Jimmy eyed them furtively. Maybe among them was the list he sought. With a quick glance about the room, he slithered to the desk. Rapidly he pawed through the papers.

A footstep sounded outside.

Moving quickly, the reporter sought refuge behind a steel locker that stood in one corner of the room. It was an instinctive move, born of surprise, but Jimmy, chuckling to himself, realized he had gained an advantageous position. From his hiding place, he might learn where the list was kept.

Coach Snelling strode into the room. Looking neither to right nor left, he walked straight ahead.

In the centre of the room he disappeared.

The reporter rubbed his eyes. Snelling had disappeared. There was no question about that, but where had he gone? Jimmy looked about the room. There was no one there.

Slowly he eased himself from behind the locker. No one hailed him.

He walked to the centre of the room. The coach had disappeared at just about that point. There seemed to be nothing unusual in sight. Standing in one spot, Jimmy slowly wheeled in a circle. Then he stopped, stock-still, frozen with astonishment.

Before him, materializing out of nothing, was a faintly outlined circular opening, large enough for a man to walk through. It looked like a tunnel, angling slightly downward from the floor level. It was into this that Coach Snelling must have walked a few moments before.

With misgivings as to the wiseness of his course, Jimmy stepped into the mouth of the tunnel. Nothing happened. He walked a few steps and stopped. Glancing back over his shoulder he could see nothing but the blurred mouth of the

20

tunnel behind him. He reached out his hands and they encountered the walls of the tunnel, walls that were hard and icy-cold.

Cautiously he moved down the tunnel, half-crouched, on the alert for danger. Within a few steps he saw another mouth to the tunnel ahead of him, only faintly outlined, giving no hint into what it might open.

Momentarily he hesitated and then plunged forward.

He stood gaping at the scene before him. He stood in a wilderness and in this wilderness, directly in front of him, was a football gridiron. Upon the field were players, garbed in gold and green uniforms, the mystery team of the Earth. On all sides of the field towered tall, gnarled oaks. Through a vista he could see a small river and beyond it blue hills fading into an indistinct horizon.

At the farther end of the field stood several tents, apparently of skins, with rudely symbolic figures painted upon them in red and yellow. Pale smoke curled up from fires in front of the tents and even where he stood Jimmy caught the acrid scent of burning wood.

Coach Snelling was striding across the field toward him and behind him trailed several copper-coloured men dressed in fringed deerskin ornamented with claws and tiny bones. One of them wore a headdress of feathers.

Jimmy had never seen an Indian. The race had died out years before. But he had seen pictures of them in historical books dealing with the early American scene. There was no doubt in his mind that he was looking upon members of the aboriginal tribes of North America.

But the coach was close now.

Jimmy mustered a smile. 'Nice hideout you have here, coach,' he said. 'Nice little place for the boys to practise without being disturbed. That tunnel had me fooled for a while.'

Coach Snelling did not return the smile. Jimmy could see the coach wasn't overjoyed at seeing him.

'So you like the place?' asked the coach.

'Sure, it's a fine place,' agreed Jimmy, feeling he was getting nowhere with this line of talk.

'How would you like to spend a few weeks here?' asked the coach, unsmilingly.

21

'Couldn't do it,' said Jimmy. 'The chief expects me back in a little while.'

Two of the brawny Indians moved forward, laid heavy hands on the reporter's shoulders.

'You're staying,' said the coach, 'until after the game.'

Hap Folsworth stepped up to the editor's desk.

'Say,' he demanded, 'did you send Russell out to get the team line-up?'

The editor looked up. 'Sure I did, just as you asked me to. Isn't that petrified newshound back yet?'

The sports-writer almost foamed at the mouth. 'Back yet!' he stormed. 'Don't you know he never gets back on time? Maybe he won't get back at all. I hear the coach is out after his blood.'

'What's the matter with the coach?'

'Russell asked him if he was going to use the same three plays this year he has used for the last ten,' explained Hap.

'I don't know what I can do,' said the editor. 'I might send one of the other boys down.'

Hap snorted. 'Mister,' he said, 'if Russell can't get the story, none of your other men can. He's the best damn reporter this sheet has ever had. But someday I'm going to kick his ribs in just to ease my feelings.'

The editor rustled papers and grumbled.

'So he's at it again,' he mused. 'Just wait until I get hold of that booze-soaked genius. I'll pickle him in a jar of *bocca* and sell him to a museum. So help me, Hannah, if I don't.'

III

Something was holding up the game. The largest football crowd ever to pack the stadium at the Martian city of Guja Tant rumbled and roared its displeasure.

The Martian team already was on the field, but the Earth team had not made its appearance.

The game would have to start soon, for it must be finished by sundown. The Terrestrial visitors, otherwise, would suffer severely from the sudden chill of Martian twilight, for although

22

the great enclosed stadium held an atmosphere under a pressure which struck a happy medium between air density on Earth and Mars, thus affording no advantage to either team, it was not equipped with heating units and the cold of the Martian night struck quickly and fiercely.

A rumour ran through the crowd.

'Something is wrong with the Earth team. Rule Eighteen. The Board of Control is holding a conference.'

A disgruntled fan grumbled.

'I knew there was something wrong when the members of the Earth team were never announced. This stuff the newspapers have been writing about a new mystery team must be right. I just thought it was some of Snelling's work, trying to scare the Martians.'

His neighbour grumbled back.

'Snelling is smart all right. But psychology won't win this ball game. He'd better have something to show us today after all that's been written about the team.'

The Martian stands shouted wild battle cries of the olden days as the Red Warriors went through their preliminary practice on the gridiron.

About the stadium lay the colourful Martian city with its weird architecture and its subtle colour blending. Beyond the city stretched the red plains, spotted here and there with the purple of occasional desert groves. The sun shone but dimly, as it always shone on the fourth planet.

'Here they come,' someone shouted.

The crowd took up the roar as the Earth team trotted out on the field, running in a long line, to swing into separate squads for the warming up period.

The roar rose and swelled, broke, ebbed lower and lower, until silence reigned over the stands.

A whistle shrilled. The officials walked out on the field. The two teams gathered. A coin flashed in the feeble sunlight. The Earth captain spoke to the referee and jerked his thumb at the north goal. The Earth team took the ball. The teams spread out.

Earth was on the defensive.

A toe smacked against the ball. The oval rose high into the air, spinning slowly. The Red Warriors thundered down the field. A Martian player cupped his arms, snared the ball.

The teams met in a swirl of action.

23

Players toppled, rolled on the ground. Like a streak of greased lightning, an Earth player cut in, flattened out in a low dive. His arms caught the ball carrier below the knees. The impact of the fall could be heard in the stands.

The teams lined up. The Martians thundered a bloodthirsty cry. The ball was snapped. Like a steel wall the Earth team rose up, smacked the Martian line flat. The back field went around the ends like thundering rockets. The carrier was caught flat-footed. Mars lost three yards on the play.

The Terrestrial fans leaped to their feet and screamed.

The teams were ready again. The ball came back. It was an end play, a twister, a puzzler. But the Earth team worked like a well-oiled machine. The runner was forced out of bounds. Mars made two yards.

Third down and eleven to go. In two tries the Red Warriors advanced the oval but five yards. Sports-writers later devoted long columns to the peculiar psychology which prevented the Martians from kicking. Perhaps, as Hap Folsworth pointed out, they were overconfident, figured that even on the fourth down they could advance the ball the necessary yardage. Perhaps, as another said, they were too stunned by the Earth defence.

The ball went to the Gold and Green.

The team shifted. The ball went back from centre. Again there was a swirl of players – sudden confusion which crystallized into an ordered pattern as an Earth ball carrier swung around right end, protected by a line of interference that moved down the charging Martians. When the Terrestrial was brought down the ball rested on the Mars twenty-yard line.

Signals. Shift. The ball was snapped. Weaving like a destroyer in heavy seas, a Green and Gold man, ball hugged to him, ploughed into the centre of the line. His team-mates opened the way for him, and even when he struck the secondary he still kept moving, ploughing ahead with pistonlike motion of his driving legs until he was hauled down by superior strength.

The ball was only two yards from the final stripe. For the first time in many years the Red Warriors were backed against their own goal line.

The Druzec war cry thundered from the Martian stands, but the Earth fans sat dumbfounded.

No one could explain the next play. Maybe there was
24

nothing to explain about it. Perhaps the Terrestrials simply charged in and by sheer force pushed the entire Martian line back for the necessary two yards. That was the way it looked.

An official raised his arms. The gigantic scoreboard clicked. Earth had scored!

The Earth stands went insane. Men and women jumped to their feet and howled their delight. The stadium shook to foot-stamping.

And throughout the entire game the Earth side of the stadium was a mad pandemonium as score after score was piled up while the Terrestrial eleven systematically ripped the Martian team apart for yard after consistent yard of ground.

The final count was 65–0 and the Earth fans, weak with triumph, came back to the realization that for four long quarters they had lived in a catapulting, rocketing, unreal world of delirious joy. For four long quarters they had made of the stadium a bedlam, a crazy, weaving, babbling, brass-tongued bedlam.

In the Martian stands sounded the long wail of lament, the death dirge of the ancient Druzecs, a lament that had not been intoned over an Earth-Mars football game for more than three-score years.

That night the Terrestrials took Guja Tant apart, such as is the right and custom of every victorious football delegation. And while the Martians may accept defeat in a philosophical manner, those who participated in the kidnapping will tell one they objected forcefully when the mascot *zimpa* – which had paraded in honour of many a Martian victory – was taken from his stable and placed on board the Earth liner chartered for the football run.

Hap Folsworth, who had covered the game for the *Evening Rocket*, explained it to Sims of the *Star* and Bradley of the *Express*.

'It's just a lot of star-dust,' he said. 'Some of Snelling's psychology. He got a bunch of big boys and he kept them under cover, taught them a lot of new tricks and built them up as a mystery team. Them Red Warriors were scared to death before they ever faced our fellows. Psychology won that game, you mark my word . . .'

Sims of the *Star* interrupted. 'Did you get a good look at any of the boys on our team?' he asked.

'Why, no, I didn't,' admitted Hap. 'Of course, I saw them out there on the field from where I was in the press section, but I didn't meet any of them face to face. The coach barred us from the dressing rooms, even after the game. That's a hell of a ways to go to win a ball game, but if he can win them that way I'm all for him.'

He puffed on a Venus-weed cigar. 'But you mark my word. It was the old psychology that turned the trick.' He stopped and looked at his two fellow sports-writers.

'Say,' exploded Hap. 'I don't think you fellows believe what I am saying.'

They didn't speak, but Hap looked at their faces again and was certain they didn't believe him.

Arthur Hart, editor of the *Evening Rocket*, looked up as the door opened.

Framed in the doorway was Jimmy Russell. Just behind him stood a copper-coloured man, naked except for a loin cloth.

The editor stared.

Men in the city room whirled around from their desks and wondered what it was all about.

'I have returned,' said Jimmy and the editor emitted a strangled yelp that knifed through the silence in the room.

The reporter walked into the room, dragging his companion after him.

'Tone down your voice,' he said, 'or you'll frighten my friend. He has seen enough in the last hour to unnerve him for a lifetime.'

'Who the hell you got there?' roared Hart.

'This gentleman,' said Jimmy, 'is Chief Hiawatha. I can't pronounce his name, so I call him Hiawatha. He lived some-where around here three, four thousand years ago.'

'This isn't a masquerade,' snapped the editor. 'This is a newspaper office.'

'Sure and I work here and I'm bringing you a story that will knock your hat off.'

'You don't mean to tell me you're bringing in the story I sent you out to get two weeks ago?' Hart purred, and his purr had an edge on it. 'You don't mean to tell me you're back already with that story.'

26

'The very same story,' agreed Jimmy.

'Too bad,' said the editor, 'but the game's over. It was over two hours ago. Earth won by a big score. I suppose you were too drunk to find that out.'

'Nothing to drink where I come from,' Jimmy told him.

'How you must have hated it,' said Hart.

'Now listen,' said Jimmy, 'do you want to get the inside story on this Earth team or don't you? I got it. And it's a big story. No wonder Earth won. Do you know that those Earth players were picked from the *best football players Earth has produced during the last 1800 years?* Why, Mars didn't have a chance!'

'Of course they didn't have a chance,' growled Hart. 'Folsworth explained all that in his story. They were licked before they started. Psychology. What's this yap about the pick of Earth teams for the past 1800 years?'

'Give me five minutes,' pleaded Jimmy, 'and if you aren't yelling yourself hoarse at the end of that time, I'll admit you're a good editor.'

'All right,' snapped the editor, 'sit down and loosen up. And you better be good or I'll fire you right out on your ear.'

'Now, Hiawatha,' said Jimmy, addressing his companion, 'you sit right down in this chair. It won't hurt you. It's a thing you rest yourself in.'

The Indian merely stared at him.

'He don't understand me very good yet,' explained Jimmy, 'but he thinks I'm a god of some sort and he does the best he can.'

Hart snorted in disgust.

'Don't snort,' cautioned the reporter. 'The poor misguided savage probably thinks you're a god, too.'

'Get going,' snarled Hart.

Jimmy seated himself on the edge of the desk. The Indian drew himself up to his full height and folded his arms across his chest. The newsmen in the room had left their desks and were crowding about.

'You see before you,' said Jimmy, 'a wild Indian, one of the aborigines of this continent. He lived here before the white men ever set foot on this land. I brought him along to show you I got the right dope.'

'What's all this got to do with the game?' persisted the editor.

'Plenty. Now you listen. You don't believe in Time travel. Neither did I until just a few days ago. There are thousands like you. Ships bridging the millions of miles of space between planets are commonplace now. Transmutation of metal is a matter of fact. Yet less than 1500 years ago people believed these things were impossible. Still, you – in this advanced age which has proven the impossible to be possible time and time again – scout the theory of Time travel along a fourth dimension. You even doubt that Time *is* a fourth dimension, or that there is such a thing possible as a fourth dimension.

'Now, just keep your shirt on!

'Nobody believes in Time travel. Let's state that as a fact. Nobody but a few fool scientists who should be turning their time and effort toward something else. Something that will spell profit, or speed up production, or make the people happier, or send space liners shooting along faster so that the Earth-Mars run can be made in just a few less minutes.

'And let me tell you that one of those fool scientists succeeded and he built a Time tunnel. I don't know what he calls it, but that describes it pretty well. I stumbled onto this thing and from what the coach told me, and what the players told, and from what the Indians tried to tell me, and from my own observations, I've got the thing all doped out. Don't ask me how the scientist made the tunnel. I don't have the least idea. I probably wouldn't understand if I met the man who made it face to face and he told me how he did it.

'Here's how the Earth team beat the Martians. The coach knew he didn't have a chance. He knew that he was in for another licking. The Earth is degenerating. Its men are getting soft. They don't measure up to the Martians. The coach looked back at the Earth players of former years and he wished he could get a few of them.'

'So,' said the editor, 'I suppose he got this Time tunnel of yours and went back and handpicked them.'

'That's exactly what he did,' declared Jimmy. 'He went over the records and he picked out the men he wanted. Then he sent his scouts back in Time and contracted them to play. He collected the whole bunch as near as I can make it out, and then he established a Time tunnel leading from his office into the past about 3,000 years and took the whole gang back there.

28

He constructed a playing field there, and he drilled men who had been dead for hundreds of years in a wilderness which existed hundreds of years before they were born. The men who played out in the Great Bowl at Guja Tant today were men who had played football before the first spaceship took to the void. Some of them have been dead for over a thousand years.

'That's what the squabble on the Control Board was about. That's what held up the game – while the Board tried to dig up something that would bar these men out of Time. But they couldn't, for the only rules of eligibility are that a man must be of unmixed Earth blood for the past ten generations and must be a football player on some college or university. And every one of those men were just that.'

Hart's eyes were stony and the reporter, looking at them, knew what to expect.

'So you would like to sit down at your old desk and write that story,' he said.

'Why not?' snarled Jimmy, ready for a battle.

'And you would like me to put it on the front page, with big green headlines, and put out an extra edition and make a big name for the *Rocket*,' Hart went on.

Jimmy said nothing. He knew nothing he could say would help.

'And you would like to make a damn fool out of me and a joke out of the *Rocket* and set in motion an athletic investigation that would have Earth and Mars on their ears for the next couple of years.'

The reporter turned to the Indian.

'Hiawatha,' he said, 'the big square-head doesn't believe us. He ought to be back burning witches at the stake. He thinks we just thought this one up.'

The Indian remained unmoved.

'Will you get the hell out of here,' snapped Hart, 'and take your friend along.'

IV

The soft, but insistent whirring of the night phone beside his bed brought the editor of the *Rocket* out of a sound sleep. He did not take kindly to night calls and when he saw the face of one of his reporters in the visaglass he growled savagely.

'What are you waking me up for?' he asked. 'You say there are fires out in the Great Bowl ... Say, do you have to call me out of bed every time a fire breaks out? Do you want me to run down there and get the story ... ? You want to know should we shoot out an extra in the morning? Say, do we put out extras every time somebody builds a bonfire, even if it is in the Great Bowl? Probably just some drunks celebrating the victory while they're waiting for the football special to come in.'

He listened as words tumbled out of the phone.

'What's that,' he shouted. 'Indians? ... Holding a war dance! How many of them? ... You say they are coming out of the administration building? ... More coming all the time, eh!'

Hart was out of bed now.

'Listen, Bob, are you certain they are Indians? ... Bill says they are, huh? Would Bill know an Indian if he saw one? ... He wasn't around this afternoon when Jim was in, was he? He didn't see that freak Jim hauled in, did he? ... If he's playing a joke, I'll crack his neck.

'Listen, Bob, you get hold of Jim. ... Yes, I know he's fired, but he'll be glad to come back again. Maybe there's something to that yarn of his. Call all the speakies and gambling joints in town. Get him if you have to arrest him. I'm coming down right away.'

Hart hauled on his clothes, grabbed a cloak and hurried to his garage, where his small service plane was stored.

A few minutes later he stamped into the *Rocket* editorial rooms.

Bob was there.

'Find Jim?' asked Hart.

'Sure, I found him.'

'What dump is he holed up in?'

'He isn't in any dump. He's out at the Bowl with the Indians. He's got hold of a half barrel of *bocca* someplace and those savages are getting ripe to tear up the place. How the Martians drink that *bocca* is beyond me. Imagine an Indian, who has never tasted alcohol, pouring it down his throat!'

'But what did Jim say ...'

'Bill got hold of him, but he won't do a thing for us. Said you insulted him.'

'I can imagine what he said,' grated Hart. 'You get Bill in here as fast as you can. Have him write a story about the Indians out at the Bowl. Call some of the other boys. Send one of them to wait for the football special and nail the coach as soon as it lands. Better have a bunch of the boys there and get interviews from the Earth players. The life story of each one of them. Shoot the works. Photographers, too. Pictures – I want hundreds of them. Find out who's been monkeying around with Time travelling and put them on the spot. Call somebody on the Control Board. See what they have to say. Get hold of the Martian coach. I'm going out to the Bowl and drag Jim back here.'

The door banged behind him and Bob grabbed for the phone.

A huge crowd had gathered at the Bowl. In the centre of the amphitheatre, on the carefully kept and tended gridiron sod, a huge bonfire blazed. Hart saw that one of the goal posts had been torn down to feed it and that piles of broken boxes were on the ground beside the fire. About the blaze leaped barbaric figures, chanting – figures snatched out of the legendry of the country's beginnings, etched against the leaping flames of the bonfire.

A murmur rose from the crowd. Hart glanced behind him.

Streaming into the Bowl came a squad of police, mounted on motor-bikes. As the squad entered the bowl they turned on the shrill blasting of the police sirens and charged full down upon the dancing figures around the fire.

Pandemonium reigned. The crowd that had gathered to watch the Indian dance scented new excitement and attempted to out-scream the sirens.

The dance halted and Hart saw the Indians draw together for a single instant, then break and run, not away from the police, but straight toward them. One savage lifted his arm. There was a glint of polished stone in the firelight as he threw the war-axe. The weapon described an arc, descended upon the head of a mounted policeman. Policeman and bike went over in a flurry of arms, legs and spinning wheels.

Above the din rose the terrible cry of the war whoop.

31

Hart saw a white man leaping ahead of the Indians, shouting at them. It was Jimmy Russell. Mad with *bocca* probably.

'Jimmy,' shrieked Hart. 'Come back here, Jimmy. You fool, come back.'

But Jimmy didn't hear. He was shouting at the Indians, urging them to follow him, straight through the charging police line, toward the administration building.

They followed him.

It was all over in a moment.

The Indians and the police met, the police swerving their machines to avoid running down the men they had been sent out to awe into submission. Then the Indians were in the clear and running swiftly after the white man who was their friend. Before the police squad could turn their charging bikes, the red-men had reached the administration building, disappeared within it.

Behind them ran Hart, his cloak whipping in the wind.

'Jimmy,' he shrieked. 'Jimmy, damn you, come back here. Everything's all right. I'll raise your salary.'

He stumbled and fell, and as he fell the police roared past him, headed for the door through which the Indians and Jimmy had disappeared.

Hart picked himself up and stumbled on. He was met at the door of the building by a police lieutenant who knew him.

'Can't understand it,' he shouted. 'There isn't a sign of them. They disappeared.'

'They're in the tunnel,' shouted Hart. 'They've gone back 3,000 years.'

The editor pushed the lieutenant to one side. But as he set foot in the building there was a dull thud, like a far-away explosion.

When he reached the coach's office he found it in ruins. The door had burst outward. The steel plates were buckled as if by a tremendous force. The furniture was upset and twisted.

Something had happened.

Hart was right. Something had happened to the Time tunnel. It had been wiped out of existence.

Alexis Androvitch spoke with a queer quirk in his voice, a half-stuttering guttural.

'But how was I to know that a foolish newspaper reporter

would go down the Time tunnel?' he demanded. 'How was I to know something would happen? What do I care for newspapers? What do I care for football games? I'll tell you. I care nothing for them. I care only for science. I do not even want to use this Time travelling personally. It would be nice to see the future, oh, yes, that would be nice – but I haven't the time. I have more work to do. I have solved Time travel. Now I care no more about it. Pouf! It is something done and finished. Now I move on. I lose interest in the possible. It is always the impossible that challenges me. I do not rest until I eliminate the impossible.'

Arthur Hart thumped the desk.

'But if you did not care about football, why did you help out Coach Snelling? Why turn over the facilities of a great discovery to an athletic coach?'

Androvitch leaned over the desk and leered at the editor.

'So you would like to know that? You would ask me that question. Well, I will tell you. Gentlemen came to me, not the coach, but other gentlemen. A gentleman by the name of Danny Carsten and others. Yes, the gangsters. Danny Carsten was killed later, but I do not care about that. I care for nothing but science.'

'Did you know who these men were when they came to you?' asked Hart.

'Certainly I knew. They told me who they were. They were very businesslike about it. They said they had heard about me working on Time travel and they asked when I thought I would have it finished. I told them I already had solved the problem and then they spread money on the table – much money, more than I had ever seen before. So I said to them: "Gentlemen, what can I do for you?" and they told me. They were frank about it. They said they wanted to win much money by betting on the game. They said they wanted me to help them get a team which would win the game. So I agreed.'

Hart leaped to his feet.

'Great galloping Jupiter,' he yelled. 'Snelling mixed up with gangsters!'

Androvitch shook his head.

'Snelling did not know he was dealing with gangsters. Others went to him and talked to him about using the Time travel method. Others he thought were his friends.'

'But, man,' said Hart, 'you aren't going to tell all this when you are called before the athletic Board of Control? There'll be an investigation that will go through the whole thing with a fine tooth comb and you'll knock Coach Snelling out of the football picture if you open your mouth about gangsters being mixed up in this.'

The scientist shook his head. 'Why should I care one way or the other. Human fortunes mean little. Progress of the race is the only thing worthwhile. I have nothing to hide. I sold the use of my discovery for money I needed to embark upon other researches. Why should I lie? If I tell the truth, maybe they will let me leave as soon as my story is told. I can't waste time at investigations. I have work to do, important work.'

'Have it your way,' said Hart, 'but the thing I came here for was to see you about Jimmy Russell. Is there any way I can reach him? Do you know what happened?'

'Something happened to the Time-control machine which was in Coach Snelling's office. It operated at all times to keep the tunnel open. It required a lot of power and we had it hooked on a high-voltage circuit. I would guess that one of the Indians, becoming frightened in the office, probably even in a drunken stupor, blundered into the machine. He more than likely tipped it over and short-circuited it. I understand fragments of human body were found in the office. Just why the tunnel or the machine should have exploded, I don't know. Electricity – just plain old electricity – was the key to the whole discovery. But probably I had set up some other type of force – let's call it a Time-force if you want to be melodramatic about it – and this force might have been responsible. There's still a lot to learn. And a lot of times a man accomplishes results which he does not suspect.'

'But what about Jimmy?'

'I'm pretty busy right now,' replied Androvitch. 'I couldn't possibly do anything for a few days . . .'

'Is there anyone else who could do the work?' asked Hart.

Androvitch shook his head. 'No other person,' he said. 'I do not confide in others. Once a Time tunnel has been established, it is easy to operate the machine – that is, projecting the Time element further away from the present or bringing it closer to the present. The football players who have been brought here to play the game were in the present time over six months. But they will be returned to their own time at approximately the same hour they left it. That merely calls for a proper adjustment of the machine controlling the tunnel back into Time. But setting up a tunnel is something only I can do. It requires considerable technique, I assure you.'

Hart brought out a bill fold. He counted out bank notes.

'Tell me when to stop,' he said.

Androvitch wet his lips and watched the notes pile up on the table before him.

Finally he raised his hand.

'I will do it,' he said. 'I will start work tomorrow.'

His hand reached out and clutched the notes.

'Thank you, Mr Hart,' he said.

Hart nodded and turned to the door. Behind him the scientist greedily counted and re-counted the bills.

V

Rush Culver shook hands with Ash Anderson, football scout for Coach August Snelling.

'I'm glad I didn't hang one on you that night you came into my room, Ash,' the fullback said. 'This has been the thrill of a lifetime. Any time you fellows need another good fullback just come back and get me.'

Anderson smiled.

'Maybe we will if the Control Board doesn't change the rules. They'll probably rip Rule Eighteen all to hell now. And all because of a lousy newspaperman who had to spill the story. No loyalty, that's what's the matter with those guys. They'd cut their grandmas' throats for a good story.'

The two stood awkwardly.

'Hate to say goodbye,' said Rush. 'One time I kind of thought I'd like to stay up ahead in your time. But there's a girl back here. And this stuff you gave me will help us get settled soon as I graduate. Right clever, the way you fellows struck off old money.'

'They'll never know the difference,' said Ash. 'They'll accept it as coin of the realm. The money we have up ahead wouldn't help you any here. As long as we had agreed to pay you, we might as well give you something you can use.'

'Well, so long, Ash,' said Culver.

'So long,' said Ash.

Rush walked slowly down the street. The music hall clock tolled the hour. Rush listened. Gone only an hour – and in that time he had lived over six months in the future. He jingled the coins in the sack he held in his hand and struck up a tune.

Then he wheeled suddenly.

'Ash – wait a minute! Ash!' he shouted.

But the man out of the future was gone.

Slowly Rush turned back down the street, heading for the house he had quitted less than 60 minutes before.

'Hell,' he said to himself, 'I forgot to thank him for helping me with my maths.'

A tiny bell tinkled softly again and again.

Arthur Hart stirred uneasily in his sleep. The bell kept on insistently. The editor sat up in bed, ran his hands through his hair and growled. The ringing continued.

'The *Morning Space-Ways*,' he said. 'Getting out an extra. Now just what in the double-dipped damnation would they be getting out an extra for?'

He pressed a lever and stepped up the intensity of the light in the room. Walking to a machine, he snapped a button and shut off the ringing bell. Opening the machine, he took from a receptacle within it a newspaper still wet with ink.

He glared at the second of the three news-delivery machines.

'If the *Star* beats the *Rocket* to an extra I'll go down and take the place apart,' he snarled. 'We been scooped too often lately. Probably isn't worth an extra, though. Just *Space-Ways* doing a little more promotion work.'

Sleepily he unfolded the sheet and glanced at the headline. It read:

TIME MACHINE
SCIENTIST SLAIN
BY GANGSTERS

Hart's breath sobbed in his throat as his eyes moved down to the second deck.

**ALEXIS ANDROVITCH TORCHED ON
STREET FROM SPEEDING CAR.
POLICE BELIEVE MARS-EARTH
GAME MAY BE CLUE.**

The *Rocket* news-delivery machine stormed into life. Another extra.

Hart snatched the paper from the machine.

He read:

**GANGSTERS SILENCE
SCIENTIST ON EVE
OF GAME HEARING**

Stunned, Hart sat down on the edge of the bed.

Androvitch was dead! The only man in the world who could set up a Time-tunnel to reach Jimmy!

It was all plain – plain as day. The gambling syndicate, afraid of what Androvitch might say, had effectively silenced him. Dead men do not talk.

Hart bowed his head in his hands.

'The best damn reporter I ever had,' he moaned.

He sprang to his feet as a thought struck him and rushed to the visaphone. Hurriedly he set up a wave length.

The face of Coach August Snelling appeared in the glass.

'Say, coach,' said Hart breathlessly, 'have you sent all the boys back to the past?'

'Hart,' said Coach Snelling in an even voice filled with cold wrath, 'after the way the newspapers have crucified me I have nothing to say.'

'But, coach,' pleaded Hart, 'I'm not asking you for publication. What you can tell me will never be printed. I want your help.'

'I needed your help the other day,' Snelling reminded him, 'and you told me news was news. You said you owed it to your readers to publish every detail of any news story.'

'But a man's life depends on this,' shouted Hart. 'One of my reporters is back in the time where you trained the team. If I could use one of the other tunnels – one of those you used to bring the boys forward in Time – I could shoot it back to the correct time. Then I could travel to where Jimmy is and bring him back . . .'

'I'm telling you the truth when I say that the boys have all been sent back and all the tunnels are closed,' Snelling said. 'The last player went back this afternoon.'

'Well,' said Hart slowly, 'I guess that settles it . . .'

Snelling interrupted. 'I heard about Russell,' he said, 'and if he's trapped back with those Indians it's what I'd call poetic justice.'

The glass went black as Snelling cut the connection.

The *Star* machine bell hammered. Hart wearily shut off the extra signal and took out the paper.

'Hell,' he said, 'if we'd had Jimmy here we'd have scooped even the *Space-Ways* on this yarn.'

He looked sadly at the three editions.

'Best damn reporter I ever knew,' the editor said.

Prof. Ebner White was lecturing to Elementary Astronomy, Section B.

'While there is reason to believe that Mars has an atmosphere,' he was saying, 'there is every reason to doubt that the planet has conditions which would allow the existence of life forms. There is little oxygen in the atmosphere, if there is an atmosphere. The red colour of the planet would argue that much of whatever oxygen may have been at one time in the atmosphere . . .'

At this point Prof. White was rudely interrupted.

A young man had risen slowly to his feet.

'Professor,' he said, 'I've listened to you for the last half hour and have reached a conclusion you know nothing about what you are saying. I can tell you that Mars does have an atmosphere. It also has plenty of oxygen and other conditions favourable to life. In fact, there is life there . . .'

The young man stopped talking, realizing what he had done. The class was on the verge of breaking into boisterous gaiety and gales of strangled guffaws swept the room. No one liked Prof. White.

The professor sputtered feebly and tried to talk. Finally he did.

'Perhaps, Mr Culver,' he suggested, 'you had better come up here while I come down and occupy your seat.'

'I'm sorry, sir. I forgot myself. It won't happen again. I publicly and sincerely apologize.'

He sat down and Prof. White went on with the lecture.

Which incident explains why Rush Culver became a tradition at the University of Wisconsin.

Marvellous tales were told of him. He was voted the man of the year in his senior year. He was elected a member of outstanding campus organizations which even his great football prowess in his junior and sophomore years had failed to obtain for him.

From a mediocre student he became regarded as a brilliant mind. Students to whom he had formerly gone for help with mathematics and other studies now came to him.

At one time he took the floor in a political science discussion hour and used up the entire hour explaining the functioning of a Utopian form of government. Those who heard him later said that he sounded as if he might have seen the government in actual operation.

But his greatest glory came from the credit which was accorded him for Wisconsin's football triumphs. Rumour on the campus said that he had worked out and given to the coach a series of plays, based upon gridiron principles then entirely new to the game. Rush, when approached, denied he had given them to the coach. But, however that may be, Wisconsin did spring upon its opponents that fall a devastating attack. Team after team fell before the onslaught of the Badgers. The team travelled to Minneapolis and there it marched through the mighty Golden Gophers with apparent ease, while fans and sports-writers grew faint with wonder and the football world trembled with amazement.

Clamorous popular demand forced the Big Ten to rescind its ruling against post-season games and at the Rose Bowl on January 1, 1945, the Badgers defeated the Trojans 49 to 0 in what sports-writers termed the greatest game ever played in football.

Jimmy Russell was up a tree. He had been lucky to find the tree, for there were few in that part of the country and at the moment he reached it, Jimmy was desperately in need of a tree.

Below him patrolled an enormous grizzly bear, fighting mad,

snarling and biting at the shafts of arrows which protruded from his shoulders. The bole of the tree was scarred and splintered where the enraged animal had struck savagely at it with huge paws armed with four-inch talons. Low limbs had been ripped from the trunk as the beast reared to his full height, attempting to reach his quarry.

In a gully a quarter of a mile away lay the ripped and torn body of Chief Hiawatha. The bear had singled the Indian out in his first charge. Jimmy had sent his last arrow winging deep into the animal's throat as the beast had torn the life from his friend. Then, without means of defence and knowing that his companion was dead, Jimmy had run, madly, blindly. The tree saved him, at least temporarily. He still had hopes that that last arrow, inflicting a deep throat wound, from which blood flowed freely, would eventually spell death to the maddened beast.

Sadly he reflected, as he perched on a large branch, that if he ever did get down alive the rest of the trip would be lonely. It was still a long way to Mexico and the Aztec civilization, but the way would not have seemed long with old Chief Hiawatha beside him. The chief had been his only friend in this savage, prehistoric world and now he lay dead and Jimmy faced another thousand miles alone, on foot, without adequate weapons.

'Maybe I should have waited at the village,' Jimmy told himself. 'Somebody might have gotten through to me. But maybe nobody wanted to get through. Funny, though, I always figured Hart was my friend, even if he did get hard-boiled every time he saw me. Still – I waited three years and that should have given him plenty of time.'

A lone buffalo bull wandered up the gully and over the ridge where the grizzly stood guard under the tree. The bear, sighting the bull, rushed at him, roaring with rage. For a moment it appeared the bull might stand his ground, but before the bear covered half the distance to him, he wheeled about and lumbered off. The grizzly came back to the tree.

Far out on the plain Jimmy located a skittering band of antelope and watched them for a long time. A wolf slunk through the long grass in a gully to the west of the tree. In the sky vultures began to wheel and turn. Jimmy shook his fist at them and cursed.

Twilight came and still the bear kept up the watch. At times he withdrew a short distance and lay down as if he were growing weak from loss of blood. But in each instance he came back to resume the march around the tree.

The moon came up and wolves howled plaintively from the ridges to the east. Jimmy, tearing a buckskin strip from his shirt, lashed himself to the tree. It was well he did so, for in spite of the danger below, despite his efforts to keep awake, he fell asleep.

The moon was low in the west when he awoke. He was stiff and chilled and for a moment he did not remember where he was.

A slinking form slipped over a ridge a short distance away and from somewhere on the prairie came the roaring grunting of a herd of awakening buffalo.

With a realization of his position coming to him, Jimmy looked about for the bear. He did not locate the beast at first, but finally saw its great bulk stretched out on the ground some distance away. He shouted, but the animal did not stir.

Late afternoon saw Jimmy heading southwest across the plains. He was clad in tattered buckskins. He was armed with a bow and a few arrows. At his belt swung a tomahawk. But he walked with a free swinging tread and his head was high.

Behind him a mound of stones marked the last resting place of all that remained mortal of Chief Hiawatha. Ahead of him lay Mexico, land of the Aztecs.

There he would find the highest order of civilization in pre-Columbian North America. There he would find people whose legends told of a strange white god who came to them in ancient days and taught them many things. This was the story they had told the Spanish conquistadores. That was why they had hailed Cortez as a god likewise, to their later sorrow.

'A white god who taught them many things,' said Jimmy to himself and chuckled. Might he not have been that white god? Could he not have taught them many things? But if he had been a god to the Aztecs, why had he not warned them against the Spaniards?

Jimmy chuckled again.

'A newspaperman should make one hell of a good god for a bunch of redskins,' he told himself.

41

JACKPOT

I found Doc in the dispensary. He had on quite a load. I worked him over some to bring him half awake.

'Get sobered up,' I ordered curtly. 'We made planetfall. We've got work to do.'

I took the bottle and corked it and set it high up on the shelf, where it wasn't right at hand.

Doc managed to achieve some dignity. 'You needn't worry, Captain. As medic of this tub . . .'

'I want all hands up and moving. We may have something out there.'

'I know,' Doc said mournfully. 'When you talk like that, it's bound to be a tough one. An off-beat climate and atmosphere pure poison.'

'It's Earth-type, oxygen, and the climate's fine so far. Nothing to be afraid of. The analysts gave it almost perfect rating.'

Doc groaned and held his head between his hands. 'Those analysts of ours do very well if they tell us whether it is hot or cold or if the air is fit to breathe. We're a haywire outfit, Captain.'

'We do all right,' I said.

'We're scavengers and sometimes birds of prey. We scour the Galaxy for anything that's loose.'

I paid no attention to him. That was the way he always talked when he had a skin full.

'You get up to the galley,' I told him, 'and let Pancake pour some coffee into you. I want you on your feet and able to do your fumbling best.'

But Doc wasn't ready to go just yet. 'What is it this time?'

'A silo. The biggest thing you ever saw. It's ten or fifteen miles across and goes up clear out of sight.'

'A silo is a building to store winter forage. Is this a farming planet?'

'No,' I said, 'it's desert. And it isn't a silo. It just looks like one.'

'Warehouse?' asked Doc. 'City? Fortress? Temple – but that doesn't make any difference to us, does it, Captain? We loot temples, too.'

'Get up!' I yelled at him. 'Get going.'

He made it to his feet. 'I imagine the populace has come out to greet us. Appropriately, I hope.'

'There's no populace,' I said. 'The silo's just standing there alone.'

'Well, well,' said Doc. 'A second-storey job.'

He started staggering up the catwalk and I knew he'd be all right. Pancake knew exactly how to get him sobered up.

I went back to the port and found that Frost had everything all set. He had the guns ready and the axes and the sledges, the coils of rope and the canteens of water and all the stuff we'd need. As second in command, Frost was invaluable. He knew what to do and did it. I don't know what I'd have done without him.

I stood in the port and looked out at the silo. We were a mile or so away from it, but it was so big that it seemed to be much closer. This near to it, it seemed to be a wall. It was just God-awful big.

'A place like that,' said Frost, 'could hold a lot of loot.'

'If it isn't empty,' I answered. 'If there isn't someone or something there to stop us taking it. If we can get into it.'

'There are openings along the base. They look like entrances.'

'With doors ten feet thick.'

I wasn't being pessimistic. I was being logical – I'd seen so many things that looked like billions turn into complicated headaches that I never allowed myself much hope until I had my hands on something I knew would bring us cash.

Hutch Murdock, the engineer, came climbing up the catwalk. As usual, he had troubles. He didn't even stop to catch his breath.

'I tell you,' he said to me, 'one of these days those engines will just simply fall apart and leave us hanging out in space light-years from nowhere. We work all the blessed time to keep them turning over.'

I clapped him on the shoulder. 'Maybe this is it. Maybe after this we can buy a brand-new ship.'

But it didn't cheer him up. He knew as well as I did that I was talking to keep up my spirit as well as his.

'Someday,' he said, 'we'll have bad trouble on our hands. Those boys of mine will drive a soap bubble across three hundred light-years if it's got an engine in it. But it's got to have an engine. And this wreck we got . . .'

He would have kept right on, but Pancake blew the horn for breakfast.

Doc was already at the table and he seemed to be functioning. He had a moderate case of shudders and he seemed a little pale. He was a little bitter, too, and somewhat poetic.

'So we gather glory,' he told us. 'We go out and lap it up. We haunt the ruins and we track the dream and we come up dripping cash.'

'Doc,' I said, 'shut up.'

He shut up. There was no one on the ship I had to speak to twice.

We didn't dally with the food. We crammed it down and left. Pancake left the dishes standing on the table and came along with us.

We got into the silo without any trouble. There were entrances all around the base and there weren't any doors. There was not a thing or anyone to stop us walking in.

It was quiet and solemn inside – and unspectacular. It reminded me of a monstrous office building.

It was all cut up with corridors, with openings off the corridors leading into rooms. The rooms were lined with what looked like filing cases.

We walked for quite a while, leaving paint markers along the walls to lead us back to the entrance. Get lost inside a place like that and one could wander maybe half a lifetime finding his way out.

We were looking for something – almost anything – but we didn't find a thing except those filing cases.

44

So we went into one of the rooms to have a look inside the files.

Pancake was disgusted. 'There won't be nothing but records in those files. Probably a lingo we can't even read.'

'There could be anything inside those files,' said Frost. 'They don't have to be records.'

Pancake had a sledge and he lifted it to smash one of the files, but I stopped him. There wasn't any use doing it messy if there was a better way.

We fooled around a while and we found the place where you had to wave your hand to make a drawer roll out.

The drawer was packed with what looked like sticks of dynamite. They were about two inches in diameter and a foot, or maybe a little more, in length, and they were heavy.

'Gold,' said Hutch.

'I never saw black gold,' Pancake said.

'It isn't gold,' I told them.

I was just as glad it wasn't. If it had been, we'd have broken our backs hauling it away. Gold's all right, but you can't get rich on it. It doesn't do much more than pay wages.

We dumped out a pile of the sticks and squatted on the floor, looking them over.

'Maybe it's valuable,' said Frost, 'but I wouldn't know. What do you think it is?'

None of us had the least idea.

We found some sort of symbols on each end of the sticks and the symbols on each stick seemed to be different, but it didn't help us any because the symbols made no sense.

We kicked the sticks out of the way and opened some more drawers. Every single drawer was filled with the sticks.

We went into some other rooms and we waved our hands some more and the drawers came popping out and we didn't find anything except more sticks.

When we came out of the silo, the day had turned into a scorcher. Pancake climbed the ladder to stack us up some grub and the rest of us sat down in the shade of the ship and laid several of the sticks out in front of us and sat there looking at them, wondering what we had.

'That's where we're at a big disadvantage,' said Hutch. 'If a regular survey crew stumbled onto this, they'd have all sorts of

45

experts to figure out the stuff. They'd test it a dozen different ways and they'd skin it alive almost and they'd have all sorts of ideas and they'd come up with some educated guesses. And pretty soon, one way or another, they'd know just what it was and if it was any use.'

'Someday,' I told them, 'if we ever strike it rich, we'll have to hire us some experts. The kind of loot we're always turning up, we could make good use of them.'

'You won't find any,' said Doc, 'that would team up with a bunch like us.'

'Where do you get "bunch-like-us" stuff?' I asked him, a little sore. 'Sure, we ain't got much education and the ship is just sort of glued together and we don't use any fancy words to cover up the fact that we're in this for all we can get out of it. But we're doing an honest job.'

'I wouldn't call it exactly honest. Sometimes we're inside the law and sometimes outside it.'

That was nonsense and Doc knew it. Mostly where we went, there wasn't any law.

'Back on Earth, in the early days,' I snapped back, 'it was folks like us who went into new lands and blazed the trails and found the rivers and climbed the mountains and brought back word to those who stayed at home. And they went because they were looking for beaver or for gold or slaves or for anything else that wasn't nailed down tight. They didn't worry much about the law or the ethics of it and no one blamed them for it. They found it and they took it and that was the end of it. If they killed a native or two or burned a village or some other minor thing like that, why, it was just too bad.'

Hutch said to Doc: 'There ain't no sense in you going holy on us. Anything we done, you're in as deep as we are.'

'Gentlemen,' said Doc, in that hammy way of his, 'I wasn't trying to stir up any ruckus. I was just pointing out that you needn't set your heart on getting any experts.'

'We could get them,' I said, 'if we offered them enough. They got to live, just like anybody else.'

'They have professional pride, too. That's something you've forgotten.'

'We got you.'

'Well, now,' said Hutch, 'I'm not too sure Doc is professional. That time he pulled the tooth for me . . .'

46

'Cut it out,' I said. 'The both of you.'

This wasn't any time to bring up the matter of the tooth. Just a couple of months ago, I'd got it quieted down and I didn't want it breaking out again.

Frost picked up one of the sticks and turned it over and over, looking at it.

'Maybe we could rig up some tests,' he suggested.

'And take the chance of getting blown up?' asked Hutch.

'It might not go off. You have a better than fifty-fifty chance that it's not explosive.'

'Not me,' said Doc. 'I'd rather just sit here and guess. It's less tiring and a good deal safer.'

'You don't get anywhere by guessing,' protested Frost. 'We might have a fortune right inside our mitts if we could only find out what these sticks are for. There must be tons of them stored in the building. And there's nothing in the world to stop us from taking them.'

'The first thing,' I said, 'is to find out if it's explosive. I don't think it is. It looks like dynamite, but it could be almost anything. For instance, it might be food.'

'We'll have Pancake cook us up a mess,' said Doc.

I paid no attention to him. He was just needling me.

'Or it might be fuel,' I said. 'Pop a stick into a ship engine that was built to use it and it would keep it going for a year or two.'

Pancake blew the chow horn and we all went in.

After we had eaten, we got to work.

We found a flat rock that looked like granite and above it we set up a tripod made out of poles that we had to walk a mile to cut and then had to carry back. We rigged up a pulley on the tripod and found another rock and tied it to the rope that went up to the pulley. Then we paid out the rope as far as it would go and there we dug a foxhole.

By this time, the sun was setting and we were tuckered out, but we decided to go ahead and make the test and set our minds at rest.

So I took one of the sticks that looked like dynamite and while the others back in the foxhole hauled up the rock tied to the rope, I put the stick on the first rock underneath the second and then I ran like hell. I tumbled into the foxhole and the others let go of the rope and the rock dropped down on the stick.

Nothing happened.

Just to make sure, we pulled up and dropped the rock two or three times more and there was no explosion.

We climbed out of the foxhole and went over to the tripod and rolled the rock off the stick, which wasn't even dented.

By this time, we were fairly well convinced that the stick couldn't be set off by concussion, although the test didn't rule out a dozen other ways it might blow us all up.

That night, we gave the sticks the works. We poured acid on them and the acid just ran off. We tried a cold chisel on them and we ruined two good chisels. We tried a saw and they stripped the teeth clean off.

We wanted Pancake to try to cook one of them, but Pancake refused.

'You aren't bringing that stuff into my galley,' he said. 'If you do, you can cook for yourselves from now on. I keep a good clean galley and I try to keep you guys well fed and I ain't having you mess up the place . . .'

'All right, Pancake,' I said. 'Even with you cooking it, it probably wouldn't be fit to eat.'

We wound up sitting at a table, looking at the sticks piled in the centre of it. Doc brought out a bottle and we all had a drink or two. Doc must have been considerably upset to share his liquor with us.

'It stands to reason,' said Frost, 'that the sticks are good for something. If the cost of that building is any indication of their value, they're worth a fortune.'

'Maybe the sticks aren't the only things in there,' Hutch pointed out. 'We just covered part of the first floor. There might be a lot of other stuff in there. And there are all those other floors. How many would you say there were?'

'Lord knows,' said Frost. 'When you're on the ground, you can't be sure you see to the top of it. It just sort of fades away when you look up at it.'

'You notice what it was built of?' asked Doc.

'Stone,' said Hutch.

'I thought so, too,' said Doc. 'But it isn't. You remember

these big apartment mounds we ran into in that insect culture out on Suud?'

We all remembered them, of course. We'd spent days trying to break into them because we had found a handful of beautifully carved jade scattered around the entrance of one of them and we figured there might be a lot of it inside. Stuff like that brings money. Folks back in civilization are nuts about any kind of alien art and that jade sure enough was alien.

We'd tried every trick that we could think of and we got nowhere. Breaking into those mounds was like punching a feather pillow. You could dent the surface plenty, but you couldn't break it because the strength of the material built up as pressure compressed the atoms. The harder you hit, the tougher it became. It was the kind of building material that would last forever and never need repair and those insects must have known they were safe from us, for they went about their business and never noticed us. That's what made it so infuriating.

And material like that, I realized, would be just the ticket for a structure like the silo. You could build as big or as high as you had a mind to; the more pressure you put on the lower structure, the stronger it would be.

'It means,' I said, 'that the building out there could be much older than it seems to be. It could be a million years or older.'

'If it's that old,' said Hutch, 'it could really be packed. You can store away a lot of loot in a million years.'

Doc and Frost drifted off to bed and Hutch and I sat there alone, looking at the sticks.

I got to thinking about some of the things that Doc was always saying about how we were just a bunch of cut-throats, and I wondered if he might be right. But think on it as hard and as honest as I could, I couldn't buy it.

On every expanding frontier, in all of history, there had been three kinds of men who went ahead and marked out the trails for other men to follow – the traders and the missionaries and the hunters.

We were the hunters in this case, hunting not for gold or slaves or furs, but for whatever we could find. Sometimes we came back with empty hands and sometimes we made a haul. Usually, in the long run, we evened out so we made nothing

49

more than wages. But we kept on going out, hoping for that lucky break that would make us billionaires.

It hadn't happened yet, and perhaps it never would. But someday it might. We touched the ghostly edge of hope just often enough to keep us thinking that it would. Although, I admitted to myself, perhaps we'd have kept going out even if there'd been no hope at all. Seeking for the unknown gets into your blood.

When you came right down to it, we probably didn't do a bit more harm than the traders or the missionaries. What we took, we took; we didn't settle down and change or destroy the civilizations of people we pretended we were helping.

I said as much to Hutch. He agreed with me.

'The missionaries are the worst,' he said. 'I wouldn't be a missionary no matter what they paid me.'

We weren't doing any good just sitting there, so I got up to start for bed.

'Maybe tomorrow we'll find something else,' I said.

Hutch yawned. 'I sure hope we do. We been wasting our time on these sticks of dynamite.'

He picked them up and on our way up to bed, he heaved them out the port.

The next day, we did find something else.

We went much deeper into the silo than we had been before, following the corridors for what must have been two miles or more.

We came to a big room that probably covered ten or fifteen acres and it was filled from wall to wall with rows of machines, all of them alike.

They weren't much to look at. They resembled to some extent a rather ornate washing machine, with a bucket seat attached and a dome on top. They weren't bolted down and you could push them around and when we tipped one of them up to look for hidden wheels, we found instead a pair of runners fixed on a swivel so they'd track in any direction that one pushed. The runners were made of metal that was greasy to the touch, but when you rubbed your fingers on them, no grease came off them.

There was no power connection.

'Maybe it's a self-powered unit,' said Frost. 'Come to think of it, I haven't noticed any power outlets in the entire building.'

*

We hunted for some place where we could turn on the power and there wasn't any place. That whole machine was the smoothest, slickest hunk of metal you ever saw. We looked for a way to get into its innards, so we could have a look at them, but there wasn't any way. The jacket that covered the works seemed to be one solid piece without an apparent seam or a sign of a bolt or rivet.

The dome looked as though it ought to come off and we tried to get it off, but it remained stubbornly in place.

The bucket seat, however, was something else again. It was lousy with all sorts of attachments to accommodate the sitting surface of almost any conceivable kind of being. We had a lot of fun adjusting it in different ways and trying to figure out what kind of animal could have a seat like that. We got a bit obscene about it, I remember, and Hutch was doubled up laughing.

But we weren't getting anywhere and we were fairly sure we wouldn't until we could get a cutting tool and open up one of the machines to find out what made it tick.

We picked out one of them and we skidded it down the corridors. When we got to the entrance, we figured we would have to carry it, but we were mistaken. It skidded along over the ground and even loose sand almost as well as it did in the corridors.

After supper, Hutch went down to the engine room and came back with a cutting tool. The metal was tough, but we finally got at least some of the jacket peeled away.

The innards of that machine were enough to drive you crazy. It was a solid mass of tiny parts all hooked together in the damnedest jumble. There was no beginning and no end. It was like one of those puzzle mazes that go on and on forever and get no place.

Hutch got into it with both hands and tried to figure out how to start taking it apart.

After a while, he sat back on his heels and growled a little at it. 'There's nothing holding them together. Not a bolt or rivet, not even so much as a cotter pin. But they hang together somehow.'

'Just pure cussedness,' I said.

He looked at me kind of funny. 'You might be right, at that.'

51

He went at it again and bashed a couple of knuckles and sat there sucking at them.

'If I didn't know that I was wrong,' he said, 'I'd say that it was friction.'

'Magnetism,' Doc offered.

'I tell you what, Doc,' said Hutch. 'You stick to what little medicine you know and let me handle the mechanics.'

Frost dove in quick to head off an argument. 'That frictional idea might not be a bad one. But it would call for perfect machining and surface polish. Theoretically, if you place two perfectly polished surfaces together, the molecules will attract one another and you'll have permanent cohesion.'

I don't know where Frost got all that stuff. Mostly he seemed to be just like the rest of us, but occasionally he'd come out with something that would catch you by surprise. I never asked him anything about himself; questions like that were just plain bad manners.

We messed around some more and Hutch bashed another knuckle and I sat there thinking how we'd found two items in the silo and both of them had stopped us in our tracks. But that's the way it is. Some days you can't make a dime.

Frost moved around and pushed Hutch out of the way. 'Let me see what I can do.'

Hutch didn't protest any. He was licked.

Frost started pushing and pulling and twisting and fiddling away at that mess of parts and all at once there was a kind of whooshing sound, like someone had let out their breath sort of slow and easy, and all the parts fell in upon themselves. They came unstuck, in a kind of slow-motion manner, and they made a metallic thump along with tinkling sounds and they were just a heap inside the jacket that had protected them.

'Now see what you done!' howled Hutch.

'I didn't do a thing,' said Frost. 'I was just seeing if I could bust one loose and one did and then the whole shebang caved in.'

He held up his fingers to show us the piece that had come loose.

'You know what I think?' asked Pancake. 'I think whoever made that machine made it so it would fall apart if anyone tried to tinker with it. They didn't want no one to find out how it was put together.'

'That makes sense,' said Doc. 'No use getting peeved at it. After all, it was their machine.'

'Doc,' I said, 'you got a funny attitude. I never noticed you turning down your share of anything we find.'

'I don't mind when we confine ourselves to what you might call, in all politeness, natural resources. I can even stomach the pillaging of art forms. But when it comes to stealing brains — and this machine is brains . . .'

Frost let out a whoop.

He was hunkered down, with his head inside the jacket of the machine, and I thought at first he'd got caught and that we'd have to cut him out, but he could get out, all right.

'I see now how to get that dome off the top,' he said.

It was a complicated business, almost like a combination on a safe. The dome was locked in place by a lot of grooves and you had to know just how to turn it to lift it out of place.

Frost kept his head inside the jacket and called out directions to Hutch, who twisted the dome first this way and then that, sometimes having to pull up on it and other times press down to engage the slotted mechanism that held it locked in place. Pancake wrote down the combinations as Frost called them off and finally the dome came loose in Hutch's hands.

Once it was off, there was no mystery to it. It was a helmet, all rigged out with adjustable features so it could be made to fit any type of head, just as the seat was adjustable to fit any sitting apparatus.

The helmet was attached to the machine with a retractable cable that reeled out far enough to reach someone sitting in the seat.

And that was fine, of course. But what was it? A portable electric chair? A permanent wave machine? Or what?

So Frost and Hutch poked around some more and in the top of the machine, just under where the dome had nested, they found a swivel trap door and underneath it a hollow tube extending into the mass of innards — only the innards weren't a mass any more, but just a basket of loose parts.

It didn't take any imagination to figure what that hollow

53

tube was for. It was just the size to take one of the sticks of dynamite.

Doc went and got a bottle and passed it around as a sort of celebration and after a drink or two, he and Hutch shook hands and said there were no hard feelings. But I didn't pay much attention to that. They'd done it many times before and then been at one another's throat before the night was over.

Just why we were celebrating was hard to figure. Sure, we knew the machine fitted heads and that the dynamite fitted the machine – but we still had no idea what it was all about.

We were, to tell the truth, just a little scared, although you couldn't have gotten one of us to admit it.

We did some guessing, naturally.

'It might be a mechanical doctor,' said Hutch. 'Just sit in that seat and put the helmet on your head and feed in the proper stick and you come out cured of whatever is wrong with you. It would be a blessing, I can tell you. You wouldn't ever need to worry if your doctor knew his business or not.'

I thought Doc was going to jump right down Hutch's throat, but he must have remembered how they had shaken hands and he didn't do it.

'As long as you're thinking along that line,' said Doc, 'let's think a little bigger. Let's say it is a rejuvenation machine and the stick is crammed with vitamins and hormones and such that turn you young again. Just take the treatment every twenty years or so and you stay young forever.'

'It might be an educator,' Frost put in. 'Those sticks might be packed full of knowledge. Maybe a complete college subject inside each of them.'

'Or it might be just the opposite,' said Pancake. 'Those sticks might soak up everything you know. Each of those sticks might be the story of one man's whole life.'

'Why record life stories?' asked Hutch. 'There aren't many men or aliens or what-not that have life stories important enough to rate all that trouble.'

'If you're thinking of it being some sort of communications deal,' I said, 'it might be anything. It might be propaganda or religion or maps or it might be no more than a file of business records.'

'And,' said Hutch, 'it might kill you deader than a mackerel.'

'I don't think so,' Doc replied. 'There are easier ways to kill a

54

person than to sit him in a chair and put a helmet on him. And it doesn't have to be a communicator.'

'There's one way to find out,' I said.

'I was afraid,' said Doc, 'we'd get around to that.'

'It's too complicated,' argued Hutch. 'No telling what trouble it may get us into. Why not drop it cold? We can blast off and hunt for something simple.'

'No!' shouted Frost. 'We can't do that!'

'I'd like to know why not,' said Hutch.

'Because we'd always wonder if we passed up the jackpot. We'd figure that maybe we gave up too quick – a day or two too quick. That we got scared out. That if we'd gone ahead, we'd be rolling in money.'

We knew Frost was right, but we batted it around some more before we would admit he was. All of us knew what we had to do, but there were no volunteers.

Finally we drew straws and Pancake was unlucky.

'Okay,' I said. 'First thing in the morning . . .'

'Morning, nothing!' wailed Pancake. 'I want to get it over with. I wouldn't sleep a wink.'

He was scared, all right, and he had a right to be. He felt just the way I would have if I'd drawn the shortest straw.

I didn't like barging around on an alien planet after dark, but we had to do it. It wouldn't have been fair to Pancake to have done otherwise. And, besides, we were all wrought up and we'd have no rest until we'd found out what we had.

So we got some flashes and went out to the silo. We tramped down the corridors for what seemed an endless time and came to the room where the machines were stored.

There didn't seem to be any difference in the machines, so we picked one at random. While Hutch got the helmet off, I adjusted the seat for Pancake and Doc went into an adjoining room to get a stick.

When we were all ready, Pancake sat down in the seat.

I had a sudden rush of imbecility.

'Look,' I said to Pancake, 'you don't need to do this.'

'Someone has to,' said Pancake. 'We got to find out somehow and this is the quickest way.'

'I'll take your place.'

Pancake called me a dirty name and he had no right to do

that, for I was only being helpful. But I called him another and we were back to normal.

Hutch put the helmet on Pancake's head and it came down so far you couldn't see his face. Doc popped the stick into the tube and the machine purred a little, starting up, then settled into silence. Not exactly silence, either – when you laid your ear against the jacket, you could hear it running.

Nothing seemed to happen to Pancake. He sat there cool and relaxed and Doc got to work on him at once, checking him over.

'His pulse has slowed a little,' Doc reported, 'and his heart action's sort of feeble, but he seems to be in no danger. His breathing is a little shallow, but not enough to worry about.'

It might not have meant a thing to Doc, but it made the rest of us uneasy. We stood around and watched and nothing happened. I don't know what we thought might happen. Funny as it sounds, I had thought that something would.

Doc kept close watch, but Pancake got no worse.

We waited and we waited. The machine kept running and Pancake sat slumped in the seat. He was as limp as a dog asleep and when you picked up his hand, you'd think his bones had melted plumb away. All the time we got more nervous. Hutch wanted to jerk the helmet off Pancake, but I wouldn't let him. No telling what might happen if we stopped the business in the middle.

It was about an hour after dawn that the machine stopped running. Pancake began to stir and we removed the helmet.

He yawned and rubbed his eyes and sat up straight. He looked a bit surprised when he saw us and it seemed to take a moment for him to recognize us.

'What happened?' Hutch asked him.

Pancake didn't answer. You could see him pulling himself together, as if he were remembering and getting his bearings once again.

'I went on a trip,' he said.

'A travelogue!' said Doc, disgusted.

'Not a travelogue. I was *there*. It was a planet, way out at the rim of the Galaxy, I think. There weren't many stars at night because it was so far out – way out where the stars get thin

56

and there aren't many of them. There was just a thin strip of light that moved overhead.'

'Looking at the Galaxy edge-on,' said Frost, nodding. 'Like you were looking at a buzz-saw's cutting edge.'

'How long was I under?' asked Pancake.

'Long enough, ' I told him. 'Six or seven hours. We were getting nervous.'

'That's funny,' said Pancake. 'I'll swear I was there for a year or more.'

'Now let's get this straight,' Hutch said. 'You say you were there. You mean you *saw* this place.'

'I mean I was *there*!' yelled Pancake. 'I *lived* with those people and I *slept* in their burrows and I *talked* with them and I *worked* with them. I got a blood blister on my hand from hoeing in a garden. I travelled from one place to another and I saw a lot of things and it was just as real as sitting here.'

We bundled him out of there and went back to the ship. Hutch wouldn't let Pancake get the breakfast. He threw it together himself and since Hutch is a lousy cook, it was a miserable meal. Doc dug up a bottle and gave Pancake a drink, but he wouldn't let any of the rest of us have any of it. Said it was medicinal, not social.

That's the way he is at times. Downright hog-selfish.

Pancake told us about this place he had been to. It didn't seem to have much, if any, government, mostly because it didn't seem to need one, but was a humble sort of planet where rather dim-witted people lived in a primitive agricultural state. They looked, he said, like a cross between a human and a groundhog, and he drew a picture of them, but it didn't help a lot, for Pancake is no artist.

He told us the kind of crops they raised, and there were some screwy kinds, and what kind of food they ate, and we gagged at some of it, and he even had some of the place names down pat and he remembered shreds of the language and it was outlandish-sounding.

We asked him all sorts of questions and he had the answers to every one of them and some were the kind he could not have made up from his head. Even Doc, who had been sceptical to start with, was ready to admit that Pancake had visited the planet.

*

After we ate, we hustled Pancake off to bed and Doc checked him over and he was all right.

When Pancake and Doc had left, Hutch said to me and Frost: 'I can feel those dollars clinking in my pocket right this minute.'

We both agreed with him.

We'd found an entertainment gadget that had anything yet known backed clear off the map.

The sticks were recordings that packed in not only sight and sound, but stimuli for all the other senses. They did the job so well that anyone subjected to their influence felt that he was part of the environment they presented. He stepped into the picture and became part of it. He was really there.

Frost already was planning exactly how we'd work it.

'We could sell the stuff,' he said, 'but that would be rather foolish. We want to keep control of it. We'll lease out the machines and we'll rent the sticks and since we'll have the sole supply, we can charge anything we wish.'

'We can advertise year-long vacations that take less than half a day,' said Hutch. 'They'll be just the thing for executives and other busy people. Why, in a single weekend you could spend four or five years' time on several different planets.'

'Maybe it's not only planets,' Frost went on. 'There might be concerts or art galleries and museums. Maybe lectures on history and literature and such.'

We were feeling pretty good, but we were tuckered out, so we trailed off to bed.

I didn't get into bed right away, however, but hauled out the log. I don't know why I ever bothered with it. It was a hit-and-miss affair at best. There would be months I'd not even think about it and then all at once I'd get all neat and orderly and keep a faithful record for several weeks or so. There was no real reason to make an entry in it now, but I was somewhat excited and had a feeling that perhaps what had just happened should be put down in black and white.

So I crawled under the bunk and pulled out the tin box I kept it and the other papers in, and while I was lifting it to the bunk, it slipped out of my hands. The lid flew open. The log and all the papers and the other odds and ends I kept there scattered on the floor.

I cussed a bit and got down on my hands and knees to pick up the mess. There was an awful lot of it and most of it was junk. Someday, I told myself, I'd have to throw a lot of it away. There were clearance papers from a hundred different ports and medical certificates and other papers that were long outdated. But among it I found also the title to the ship.

I sat there thinking back almost twenty years to the day I'd bought the ship for next to nothing and towed it from the junkyard and I recalled how I'd spent a couple of years' spare time and all I could earn getting it patched up so it could take to space again. No wonder, I told myself, that it was a haywire ship. It had been junk to start with, and during all those years, we'd just managed to keep it glued together. There had been many times when the only thing that got it past inspection had been a fast bribe slipped quietly to the man. No one in the Galaxy but Hutch could have kept it flying.

I went on picking up the papers, thinking about Hutch and all the rest of them. I got a little sentimental and thought a lot of things I'd have clobbered anyone for if they had dared to say them to me. About how we had stuck together and how any one of them would have died for me and I for any one of them.

There had been a time, of course, when it had not been that way, back in the days when they'd first signed on and had been nothing but a crew. But that day was long past; now they were more than just a crew. There had been no signing on for years, but just staying on as men who had a right to stay. And I sat there, flat on the floor, and thought how we'd finally done the thing we'd always hoped to do, how we'd caught up with the dream – us, the ragamuffin crew in the glued-together ship – and I felt proud and happy, not for myself alone, but for Hutch and Pancake and Doc and Frost and all the rest.

Finally I got the papers all picked up and back in the box again and tried to write up the log, but was too tired to write, so I went to bed, as I should have done in the first place.

But tired as I was, I lay there and thought of how big the silo was and tried to estimate how many sticks might be cached away there. I got up into the trillions and I saw it was no use; there was no way to keep the figures straight.

The whole deal was big – bigger than anything we'd ever found before. It would take a group of men like us at least five lifetimes of steady hauling to empty the silo. We'd have to set up a corporation and get a legal staff (preferably one with the lowest kind of ethics) and file a claim on this planet and go through a lot of other red tape to be sure we had it all sewed up.

We couldn't take a chance of letting it slip through our fingers because of any lack of foresight. We'd have to get it all doped out before we went ahead.

I don't know about the rest of them, but I dreamed that night of wading knee-deep through a sea of crisp, crinkly banknotes.

When morning came, Doc failed to show up for breakfast. I went hunting him and found he hadn't even gone to bed. He was sprawled in his rickety old chair in the dispensary and there was one empty bottle on the floor and he trailed another, almost empty, alongside the chair, keeping a rather flimsy hold upon its neck. He still was conscious, which was about the most that could be said of him.

I was plenty sore. Doc knew the rules. He could get paralysed as soon or as often or as long as he wanted to when we were in space, but when we were grounded and there was work to do and planet ailments to keep an eye out for, he was expected to stay sober.

I kicked the bottle out of his fist and I took him by the collar with one hand and by the seat of his britches with the other and frog-walked him to the galley.

Plunking him down in a chair, I yelled for Pancake to get another pot of coffee going.

'I want you sobered up,' I told Doc, 'so you can go out with us on the second trip. We need all the manpower we have.'

Hutch had rounded up his gang and Frost had got the crew together and had rigged up a block and tackle so we could start loading. Everyone was ready to begin bringing in the cargo except Doc and I swore to myself that, before the day was over, I'd work the tail right off him.

As soon as we had breakfast, we started out. We planned to get aboard as many of the machines as we could handle and to fill in the space between them with all the sticks we could find room for.

We went down the corridors to the room that held the machines and we paired off, two men to the machine, and started out. Everything went fine until we were more than halfway across the stretch of ground between the building and the ship.

Hutch and I were in the lead and suddenly there was an explosion in the ground about fifty feet ahead of us.

We skidded to a halt.

'It's Doc!' yelled Hutch, grabbing for his belt-gun.

I stopped him just in time. 'Take it easy, Hutch.'

Doc stood up in the port and waved a rifle at us.

'I could pick him off,' Hutch said.

'Put back that gun,' I ordered.

I walked out alone to where Doc had placed his bullet.

He lifted his rifle and I stopped dead still. He'd probably miss, but even so, the kind of explosive charge he was firing could cut a man in two if it struck ten feet away.

'I'm going to throw away my gun,' I called out to him. 'I want to talk with you.'

Doc hesitated for a moment. 'All right. Tell the rest of them to pull back a way.'

I spoke to Hutch over my shoulder. 'Get out of here. Take the others with you.'

'He's crazy drunk,' said Hutch. 'No telling what he'll do.'

'I can handle him,' I said, sounding surer than I felt.

Doc let loose another bullet off to one side of us.

'Get moving, Hutch.' I didn't dare look back. I had to keep an eye on Doc.

'All right,' Doc finally yelled at me. 'They're back. Throw away your gun.'

Moving slow so he wouldn't think I was trying to draw on him, I unfastened the buckle of the gun-belt and let it fall to the ground. I walked forward, keeping my eyes on Doc, and all the time my skin kept trying to crawl up my back.

'That's far enough,' Doc said when I'd almost reached the ship. 'We can talk from here.'

'You're drunk,' I told him. 'I don't know what this is all about, but I know you're drunk.'

'Not nearly drunk enough. Not drunk enough by half. If I were drunk enough, I simply wouldn't care.'

'What's eating you?'

'Decency,' said Doc, in that hammy way of his. 'I've told you many times that I can stomach looting when it involves no

61

more than uranium and gems and other trash like that. I can even shut my eyes when you gut a culture, because you can't steal a culture – even when you get through looting it, the culture still is there and can build back again. But I balk at robbing knowledge. I will not let you do it, Captain.'

'I still say you're drunk.'

'You don't even know what you've found. You are so blind and greedy that you don't recognize it.'

'Okay, Doc,' I said, trying to smooth his feathers, 'tell me what we've found.'

'A library. Perhaps the greatest, most comprehensive library in all the Galaxy. Some race spent untold years compiling the knowledge that is in that building and you plan to take it and sell it and scatter it. If that happens, in time it will be lost and what little of it may be left will be so out of context that half its meaning will be lost. It doesn't belong to us. It doesn't even belong to the human race alone. A library like that can belong only to all the peoples of the Galaxy.'

'Look, Doc,' I pleaded, 'we've worked for years, you and I and all the rest of them. We've bled and sweated and been disappointed time and time again. This is our chance to make a killing. And that means you as well as the rest of us. Think of it, Doc – more money than you can ever spend – enough to keep you drunk the rest of your life!'

Doc swung the rifle around at me and I thought my goose was cooked. But I never moved a muscle.

I stood and bluffed it out.

At last, he lowered the gun. 'We're barbarians. History is full of the likes of us. Back on Earth, the barbarians stalled human progress for a thousand years when they burned and scattered the libraries and the learning of the Greeks and Romans. To them, books were just something to start a fire with or wipe their weapons on. To you, this knowledge means nothing more than something to make a quick buck on. You'll take a scholarly study of a vital social problem and retail it as a year's vacation that can be experienced in six hours' time and you'll take . . .'

'Spare me the lecture, Doc,' I said wearily. 'Tell me what you want.'

62

'Go back and report this find to the Galactic Commission. It will help wipe out a lot of things we've done.'

'So help me, Doc, you've gone religious on us.'

'Not religious. Just decent.'

'And if we don't?'

'I've got the ship,' said Doc. 'I have the food and water.'

'You'll have to sleep.'

'I'll close the port. Just try getting in.'

He had us and he knew he did. Unless we could figure out a way to grab him, he had us good and proper.

I was scared, but mostly I was burned. For years, we'd listened to him run off at the mouth and never for a moment had any of us thought he meant a word of it. And now suddenly he did – he meant every word of it.

I knew there was no way to talk him out of it. And there was no compromise. When it came right down to it, there was no agreement possible, for any agreement or compromise would have to be based on honour and we had no honour – not a one of us, not even among ourselves. It was stalemate, but Doc didn't know that yet. He'd realize it once he got a little sober and thought about it some. What he had done had been done on alcoholic impulse, but that didn't mean he wouldn't see it through.

One thing was certain: As it stood, he could outlast us.

'Let me go back,' I said. 'I'll have to talk this over with the others.'

I think that Doc right then began to suspect how deeply he had become committed, began to see for the first time the impossibility of us trusting one another.

'When you come back,' he told me, 'have it all thought out. I'll want some guarantees.'

'Sure, Doc,' I said.

'I mean this, Captain. I'm in deadly earnest. I'm not just fooling.'

'I know you aren't, Doc.'

I went back to where the others were clustered just a short distance from the building. I explained what was up.

'We'll have to spread out and charge him,' Hutch decided. 'He may get one or two of us, but we can pick him off.'

'He'll simply close the port,' I said. 'He could starve us out.

In a pinch, he could try to take the ship up. If he ever managed to get sober, he could probably do it.'

'He's crazy,' said Pancake. 'Just plain drunken crazy.'

'Sure he is,' I said, 'and that makes him twice as deadly. He's been brooding on this business for a long, long time. He built up a guilt complex that is three miles high. And worst of all, he's got himself out on a limb and he can't back down.'

'We haven't got much time,' said Frost. 'We've got to think of something. A man can die of thirst. You can get awfully hungry in just a little while.'

The three of them got to squabbling about what was best to do and I sat down on the sand and leaned back against one of the machines and tried to figure Doc.

Doc was a failure as a medic; otherwise he'd not have tied up with us. More than likely, he had joined us as a gesture of defiance or despair – perhaps a bit of both. And besides being a failure, he was an idealist. He was out of place with us, but there'd been nowhere else to go, nothing else to do. For years, it had eaten at him and his values got all warped and there's no place better than deep space to get your values warped.

He was crazy as a coot, of course, but a special kind of crazy. If it hadn't been so ghastly, you might have called it glorious crazy.

You wanted to laugh him off or brush him to one side, for that was the kind of jerk he was, but he wouldn't laugh or brush.

I don't know if I heard a sound – a footstep, maybe – or if I just sensed another presence, but all at once I knew we'd been joined by someone.

I half got up and swung around toward the building and there, just outside the entrance, stood what looked at first to be a kind of moth made up in human size.

I don't mean it was an insect – it just had the look of one. Its face was muffled up in a cloak it wore and it was not a human face and there was a ruff rising from its head like those crests you see on the helmets in the ancient plays.

Then I saw that the cloak was not a cloak at all, but a part of the creature, and it looked like it might be folded wings, but it wasn't wings.

'Gentlemen,' I said as quietly as I could, 'we have a visitor.'

I walked toward the creature soft and easy and alert, not wanting to frighten it, but all set to take evasive action if it tried to put the finger on me.

'Be ready, Hutch,' I said.

'I'm covering you,' Hutch assured me and it was a comfort to know that he was there. A man couldn't get into too much trouble with Hutch backing him.

I stopped about six feet from the creature and he didn't look as bad close up as he did at a distance. His eyes seemed to be kind and gentle and his funny face, alien as it was, had a sort of peacefulness about it. But even so, you can't always tell with aliens.

We stood there looking at one another. The both of us understood there was no use of talking. We just stood and sized one another up.

Then the creature took a couple of steps and reached out a hand that was more like a claw than a hand. He took my hand in his and tugged for me to come.

There were just two things to do – either snatch my hand away or go.

I went.

I didn't stop to get it figured out, but there were several factors that helped make up my mind. First off, the creature seemed to be friendly and intelligent. And Hutch and all the others were there, just behind me. And over and above all, you don't get too far with aliens if you act stand-offish.

So I went.

We walked into the silo and behind me I heard the tramping feet of the others and it was a sound that was good to hear.

I didn't waste any time wondering where the creature might have come from. I admitted to myself, as I walked along, that I had been half-expecting something just like this. The silo was so big that it could hold many things, even people or creatures, we could not know about. After all, we'd explored only one small corner of the first floor of it. The creature, I figured, must have come from somewhere on the upper floors as soon as he learned about us. It might have taken quite a while, one way or another, for the news to reach him.

He led me up three ramps to the fourth floor of the building and went down a corridor for a little way, then went into a room.

It was not a large room. It held just one machine, but this one was a double model; it had two bucket seats and two helmets. There was another creature in the room.

The first one led me over to the machine and motioned for me to take one of the seats.

I stood there for a while, watching Hutch and Pancake and Frost and all of the others crowd into the place and line up against the wall.

Frost said: 'A couple of you boys better stay outside and watch the corridor.'

Hutch asked me: 'You going to sit down in that contraption, Captain?'

'Why not?' I said. 'They seem to be all right. There's more of us than them. They don't mean us any harm.'

'It's taking a chance,' said Hutch.

'Since when have we stopped taking chances?'

The creature I had met outside had sat down in one of the seats, so I made a few adjustments in the other. While I was doing this, the second creature went to a file and got out two sticks, but these sticks were transparent instead of being black. He lifted off the helmets and inserted the two sticks. Then he fitted one of the helmets on his fellow-creature's head and held out the other to me.

I sat down and let him put it on and suddenly I was squatting on the floor across a sort of big coffee-table from the gent I had met outside.

'Now we can talk,' said the creature, 'which we couldn't do before.'

I wasn't scared or flustered. It seemed just as natural as if it had been Hutch across the table.

'There will be a record made of everything we say,' said the creature. 'When we are finished, you will get one copy and I will get the other for our files. You might call it a pact or a contract or whatever term seems to be most applicable.'

'I'm not much at contracts,' I told him. 'There's too much legal flypaper tied up with most of them.'

'An agreement, then,' the creature suggested. 'A gentlemen's agreement.'

'Good enough,' I said.

Agreements are convenient things. You can break them any time you want. Especially gentlemen's agreements.

'I suppose you have figured out what this place is,' he said.

'Well, not for sure,' I replied. 'Library is the closest that we have come.'

'It's a university, a galactic university. We specialize in extension or home-study courses.'

I'm afraid I gulped a bit. 'Why, that's just fine.'

'Our courses are open to all who wish to take them. There are no entrance fees and there is no tuition. Neither are there any scholastic requirements for enrolment. You yourself can see how difficult it would be to set up such requirements in a galaxy where there are many races of varying viewpoints and abilities.'

'You bet I can.'

'The courses are free to all who can make use of them,' he said. 'We do expect, of course, that they make proper use of them and that they display some diligence in study.'

'You mean anyone at all can enrol?' I asked. 'And it don't cost anything?'

After the first disappointment, I was beginning to see the possibilities. With bona fide university educations for the taking, it would be possible to set up one of the sweetest rackets that anyone could ask for.

'There's one restriction,' the creature explained. 'We cannot, obviously, concern ourselves with individuals. The paperwork would get completely out of hand. We enrol cultures. You, as a representative of your culture – what is it you call yourselves?'

'The human race, originally of the planet Earth, now covering some half million cubic light-years. I'd have to see your chart . . .'

'That's not necessary at the moment. We would be quite happy to accept your application for the entrance of the human race.'

It took the wind out of me for a minute. I wasn't any representative of the human race. And if I could be, I wouldn't. This was my deal, not the human race's. But I couldn't let him know that, of course. He wouldn't have done business with me.

'Now not so fast,' I pleaded. 'There's a question or two I'd like to have you answer. What kind of courses do you offer? What kind of electives do you have?'

'First there is the basic course,' the creature said. 'It is more or less a familiarization course, a sort of orientation. It includes those subjects which we believe can be of the most use to the race in question. It is, quite naturally, tailored specifically for each student culture. After that, there is a wide field of electives, hundreds of thousands of them.'

'How about final exams and tests and things like that?' I wanted to know.

'Oh, surely,' said the creature. 'Such tests are conducted every – tell me about your time system.'

I told him the best I could and he seemed to understand.

'I'd say,' he finally said, 'that about every thousand years of your time would come fairly close. It is a long-range pro-gramme and to conduct tests any oftener would put some strain upon our resources and might be of little value.'

That decided me. What happened a thousand years from now was no concern of mine.

I asked a few more questions to throw him off the track – just in case he might have been suspicious – about the history of the university and such.

I still can't believe it. It's hard to conceive of any race working a million years to set up a university aimed at the eventual education of an entire galaxy, travelling to all the planets to assemble data, compiling the records of countless cultures, correlating and classifying and sorting out that mass of information to set up the study courses.

It was just too big for a man to grasp.

For a while, he had me reeling on the ropes and faintly starry-eyed about the whole affair. But then I managed to snap back to normal.

'All right, Professor,' I said, 'you can sign us up. What am I supposed to do?'

'Not a thing,' he said. 'The recording of our discussion will supply the data. We'll outline the course of basic study and you then may take such electives as you wish.'

'If we can't haul it all in one trip, we can come back again?' I asked.

'Oh, definitely. I anticipate you may wish to send a fleet to carry all you need. We'll supply sufficient machines and as many copies of the study recordings as you think you will need.'

'It'll take a lot,' I said bluntly, figuring I'd start high and haggle my way down. 'An awful lot.'

'I am aware of that,' he told me. 'Education for an entire culture is no simple matter. But we are geared for it.'

So there we had it – all legal and airtight. We could get anything we wanted and as much as we wanted and we'd have a right to it. No one could say we stole it. Not even Doc could say that.

The creature explained to me the system of notation they used on the recording cylinders and how the courses would be boxed and numbered so they could be used in context. He promised to supply me with recordings of the electives so I could pick out what we wanted.

He was real happy about finding another customer and he proudly told me of all the others that they had and he held forth at length on the satisfaction that an educator feels at the opportunity to pass on the torch of knowledge.

He had me feeling like a heel.

Then we were through and I was sitting in the seat again and the second creature was taking the helmet off my head.

I got up and the first creature rose to his feet and faced me. We couldn't talk any more than we could to start with. It was a weird feeling, to face a being you've just made a deal with and not be able to say a single word that he can understand.

But he held out both his hands and I took them in mine and he gave my hands a friendly squeeze.

'Why don't you go ahead and kiss him?' asked Hutch. 'Me and the boys will look the other way.'

Ordinarily, I'd have slugged Hutch for a crack like that, but I didn't even get sore.

The second creature took the two sticks out of the machine and handed one to me. They'd gone in transparent, but they came out black.

'Let's get out of here,' I said.

We got out as fast as we could and still keep our dignity – if you could call it that.

*

Outside the silo, I got Hutch and Pancake and Frost together and told them what had happened.

'We got the Universe by the tail,' I said, 'with a downhill pull.'

'What about Doc?' asked Frost.

'Don't you see? It's just the kind of deal that would appeal to him. We can let on we're noble and big-hearted and acting in good faith. All I need to do is get close enough to grab him.'

'He won't even listen to you,' said Pancake. 'He won't believe a word you say.'

'You guys stay right here,' I said. 'I'll handle Doc.'

I walked back across the stretch of ground between the building and the ship. There was no sign of Doc. I was all set to holler for him, then thought better of it. I took a chance and started up the ladder. I reached the port and there was still no sign of him.

I moved warily into the ship. I thought I knew what had become of him, but there was no need to take more chances than I had to.

I found him in his chair in the dispensary. He was stiffer than a goat. The gun lay on the floor. There were two empty bottles beside the chair.

I stood and looked at him and knew what had happened. After I had left, he had got to thinking about the situation and had run into the problem of how he'd climb down off that limb and he had solved it the way he'd solved most of his problems all his life.

I got a blanket and covered him. Then I rummaged around and found another bottle. I uncorked it and put it beside the chair, where he could reach it easy. Then I picked up the gun and went to call the others in.

I lay in bed that night and thought about it and it was beautiful.

There were so many angles that a man didn't know quite where to start.

There was the university racket which, queerly enough, was entirely legitimate, except that the professor out in the silo never meant it to be sold.

And there was the quickie vacation deal, offering a year or two on an alien planet in six hours of actual time. All we'd need to do was pick a number of electives in geography or social science or whatever they might call it.

There could be an information bureau or a research agency, charging fancy prices to run down facts on any and all subjects.

Without a doubt, there'd be some on-the-spot historical recordings and with those in hand, we could retail adventure, perfectly safe adventure, to the stay-at-homes who might hanker for it.

I thought about that and a lot of other things which were not quite so sure, but at least probable and worth investigating, and I thought, too, about how the professors had finally arrived at what seemed to me a sure-fire effective medium for education.

You wanted to know about a thing, so you up and lived it; you learned it on the ground. You didn't read about it or hear about it or even see it in plain three-dimension – you experienced it. You walked the soil of the planet you wanted to know about; you lived with the beings that you wished to study; you saw as an eyewitness, and perhaps as a participant, the history that you sought to learn.

And it could be used in other ways as well. You could learn to build anything, even a space-ship, by actually building one. You could learn how an alien machine might operate by putting it together, step by simple step. There was no field of knowledge in which it would not work – and work far better than standard educational methods.

Right then and there, I made up my mind we'd not release a single stick until one of us had previewed it. No telling what a man might find in one of them that could be put to practical use.

I fell asleep dreaming about chemical miracles and new engineering principles, of better business methods and new philosophic concepts. And I even figured out how a man could make a mint of money out of a philosophic concept.

We were on top of the Universe for sure. We'd set up a corporation with more angles than you could shake a stick at. We would be big time. In a thousand years or so, of course, there'd be a reckoning, but none of us would be around to take part in it.

*

Doc sobered up by morning and I had Frost heave him in the brig. He wasn't dangerous any longer, but I figured that a spell in pokey might do him a world of good. After a while, I intended to talk to him, but right at the moment I was much too busy to be bothered with him.

I went over to the silo with Hutch and Pancake and had another session with the professor on the double-seat machine and picked out a batch of electives and settled various matters.

Other professors began supplying us with the courses, all boxed and labelled, and we set the crew and the engine gang to work hauling them and the machines aboard and stowing them away.

Hutch and I stood outside the silo and watched the work go on.

'I never thought,' said Hutch, 'that we'd hit the jackpot this way. To be downright honest with you, I never thought we'd hit it. I always thought we'd just go on looking. It goes to show how wrong a man can be.'

'Those professors are soft in the head,' I said. 'They never asked me any questions. I can think of a lot they could have asked that I couldn't answer.'

'They're honest and think everyone's the same. That's what comes of getting so wrapped up in something you have time for nothing else.'

And that was true enough. The professor race has been busy for a million years doing a job it took a million years to do – and another million and a million after that – and that never would be finished.

'I can't figure why they did it,' I said. 'There's no profit in it.'

'Not for them,' said Hutch, 'but there is for us. I tell you, Captain, it takes brains to work out the angles.'

I told him what I had figured out about previewing everything before we gave it out, so we would be sure we let nothing slip away from us.

Hutch was impressed. 'I'll say this for you, Captain – you don't miss a bet. And that's the way it should be. We might as well milk this deal for every cent it's worth.'

'I think we should be methodical about this previewing business,' I said. 'We should start at the beginning and go straight through to the end.'

Hutch said he thought so, too. 'But it will take a lot of time,' he warned me.

'That's why we should start right now. The orientation course is on board already and we could start with that. All we'd have to do is set up a machine and Pancake could help you with it.'

'Help me!' yelled Hutch. 'Who said anything about me doing it? I ain't cut out for that stuff. You know yourself I never do any reading . . .'

'It isn't reading. You just live it. You'll be having fun while we're out here slaving.'

'I won't do it.'

'Now look,' I said, 'let's use a little sense. I should be out here at the silo seeing everything goes all right and close at hand so I can hold a powwow with the professor if there's any need of it. We need Frost to superintend the loading. And Doc is in the clink. That leaves you and Pancake. I can't trust Pancake with that previewing job. He's too scatter-brained. He'd let a fortune glide right past him without recognizing it. Now you're a fast man with a buck and the way I see it . . .'

'Since you put it that way,' said Hutch, all puffed up, 'I suppose I *am* the one who should be doing it.'

That evening, we were all dog-tired, but we felt fine. We had made a good start with the loading and in a few more days would be heading home.

Hutch seemed to be preoccupied at supper. He fiddled with his food. He didn't talk at all and he seemed like a man with something on his mind.

As soon as I could, I cornered him.

'How's it going, Hutch?'

'Okay,' he said. 'Just a lot of gab. Explaining what it's all about. Gab.'

'Like what?'

'Some of it is hard to tell. Take a lot of explaining I haven't got the words for. Maybe one of these days you'll find the time to run through it yourself.'

'You can bet your life I will,' I said, somewhat sore at him.

'There's nothing worth a dime in it so far,' said Hutch.

I believed him on that score. Hutch could spot a dollar twenty miles away.

I went down to the brig to see Doc. He was sober. Also unrepentant.

'You outreached yourself this time,' he said. 'That stuff isn't yours to sell. There's knowledge in that building that belongs to the Galaxy – for free.'

I explained to him what had happened, how we'd found the silo was a university and how we were taking the courses on board for the human race after signing up for them all regular and proper. I tried to make it sound as if we were being big, but Doc wouldn't buy a word of it.

'You wouldn't give your dying grandma a drink of water unless she paid you in advance,' he said. 'Don't give me any of that guff about service to humanity.'

So I left him to stew in the brig a while and went up to my cabin. I was sore at Hutch and all burned up at Doc and my tail was dragging. I fell asleep in no time.

The work went on for several days and we were almost finished.

I felt pretty good about it. After supper, I climbed down the ladder and sat on the ground beside the ship and looked across at the silo. It still looked big and awesome, but not as big as that first day – because now it had lost some of its strangeness and even the purpose of it had lost some of its strangeness, too.

Just as soon as we got back to civilization, I promised myself, we'd seal the deal as tight as possible. Probably we couldn't legally claim the planet because the professors were intelligent and you can't claim a planet that has intelligence, but there were plenty of other ways we could get our hooks into it for keeps.

I sat there and wondered why no one came down to sit with me, but no one did, so finally I clambered up the ladder.

I went down to the brig to have a word with Doc. He still was unrepentant, but he didn't seem too hostile.

'You know, Captain,' he said, 'there have been times when I've not seen eye to eye with you, but despite that I've respected you and sometimes even liked you.'

'What are you getting at?' I asked him. 'You can't soft-talk yourself out of the spot you're in.'

'There's something going on and maybe I should tell you.

You are a forthright rascal. You don't even take the trouble to deny you are. You have no scruples and probably no morals, and that's all right, because you don't pretend to have. You are . . .'

'Spit it out! If you don't tell me what is going on, I'll come in there and wring it out of you.'

'Hutch has been down here several times,' said Doc, 'inviting me to come up and listen to one of those recordings he is fooling with. Said it was right down my alley. Said I'd not be sorry. But there was something wrong about it. Something sneaky.' He stared round-eyed through the bars at me. 'You know, Captain, Hutch was never sneaky.'

'Well, go on!'

'Hutch has found out something, Captain. If I were you, I'd be finding out myself.'

I didn't even wait to answer him. I remembered how Hutch had been acting, fiddling with his food and preoccupied, not talking very much. And come to think of it, some of the others had been acting strangely, too. I'd just been too busy to give it much attention.

Running up the catwalks, I cussed with every step I took. A captain of a ship should never get so busy that he loses touch – he has to stay in touch all the blessed time. It had all come of being in a hurry, of wanting to get loaded up and out of there before something happened.

And now something had happened. No one had come down to sit with me. There'd not been a dozen words spoken at the supper table. Everything felt deadly wrong.

Pancake and Hutch had rigged up the chart room for the previewing chore and I busted into it and slammed the door and stood with my back against it.

Not only Hutch was there, but Pancake and Frost as well and, in the machine's bucket seat, a man I recognized as one of the engine gang.

I stood for a moment without saying anything, and the three of them stared back at me. The man with the helmet on his head didn't notice – he wasn't even there.

'All right, Hutch,' I said, 'come clean. What is all this about? Why is that man previewing? I thought just you and . . .'

'Captain,' said Frost, 'we were about to tell you.'

'You shut up! I am asking Hutch.'

'Frost is right,' said Hutch. 'We were all set to tell you. But you were so busy and it came a little hard . . .'

'What is hard about it?'

'Well, you had your heart all set to make yourself a fortune. We were trying to find a way to break it to you gentle.'

I left the door and walked over to him.

'I don't know what you're talking about,' I said, 'but we still make ourselves a killing. There never was a time of day or night, Hutch, that I couldn't beat your head in and if you don't want me to start, you better talk real fast.'

'We'll make no killing, Captain,' Frost said quietly. 'We're taking this stuff back, and we'll turn it over to the authorities.'

'All of you are nuts!' I roared. 'For years, we've slaved and sweated, hunting for the jackpot. And now that we have it in our mitts, now that we can walk barefooted through a pile of thousand-dollar bills, you are going chicken on me. What's . . .'

'It's not right for us to do it, sir,' said Pancake.

And that 'sir' scared me more than anything that had happened so far. Pancake had never called me that before.

I looked from one to the other of them and what I saw in their faces chilled me to the bone. Every single one of them thought just the same as Pancake.

'That orientation course!' I shouted.

Hutch nodded. 'It explained about honesty and honour.'

'What do you scamps know about honesty and honour?' I raged. 'There ain't one of you that ever drew an honest breath.'

'We never knew about it before,' said Pancake, 'but we know about it now.'

'It's just propaganda! It's just a dirty trick the professors played on us!'

And it *was* a dirty trick. Although you have to admit the professors knew their onions. I don't know if they figured us humans for a race of heels or if the orientation course was just normal routine. But no wonder they hadn't questioned me. No wonder they'd made no investigation before handing us their knowledge. They had us stopped before we could even make a move.

'We felt that since we had learned about honesty,' said Frost, 'it was only right the rest of the crew should know. It's an awful kind of life we've been leading, Captain.'

'So,' said Hutch, 'we been bringing in the men, one by one, and orienting them. We figured it was the least that we could do. This man is about the last of them.'

'A missionary,' I said to Hutch. 'So that is what you are. Remember what you told me one night? You said you wouldn't be a missionary no matter what they paid you.'

'There's no need of that,' Frost replied coldly. 'You can't shame us and you can't bully us. We know we are right.'

'But the money! What about the corporation? We had it all planned out!'

Frost said: 'You might as well forget it, Captain. When you take the course . . .'

'I'm not taking any course.' My voice must have been as deadly as I felt, for not a one of them made a move toward me. 'If any of you mealy-mouthed missionaries feel an urge to make me, you can start trying right now.'

They still didn't move. I had them bluffed. But there was no point in arguing with them. There was nothing I could do against that stone wall of honesty and honour.

I turned my back on them and walked to the door. At the door I stopped. I said to Frost: 'You better turn Doc loose and give him the cure. Tell him it's all right with me. He has it coming to him. It will serve him right.'

Then I shut the door behind me and went up the catwalk to my cabin. I locked the door, a thing I'd never done before.

I sat down on the edge of the bunk and stared at the wall and thought.

There was just one thing they had forgotten. This was my ship, not theirs. They were just the crew and their papers had run out long ago and never been renewed.

I got down on my hands and knees and hauled out the tin box I kept the papers in. I went through it systematically and sorted out the papers that I needed – the title to the ship and the registry and the last papers they had signed.

I laid the papers on the bunk and shoved the box out of the way and sat down again.

I picked up the papers and shuffled them from one hand to the other.

I could throw them off the ship any time I wished. I could take off without them and there was nothing, absolutely nothing, they could do about it.

And what was more, I could get away with it. It was legal, of course, but it was a rotten thing to do. Now that they were honest men and honourable, though, they'd bow to the legality and let me get away with it. And in such a case, they had no one but themselves to thank.

I sat there for a long time thinking, but my thoughts went round and round and mostly had to do with things out of the past – how Pancake had gotten tangled up in the nettle patch out in the Coonskin System and how Doc had fallen in love with (of all things) a tri-sexual being that time we touched at Siro and how Hutch had cornered the liquor supply at Munko, then lost it in a game that was akin to craps except the dice were queer little living entities that you had no control of, which made it tough on Hutch.

A rap came at the door.

It was Doc.

'You all full of honesty?' I asked him.

He shuddered. 'Not me. I turned down the offer.'

'It's the same kind of swill you were preaching at me just a couple of days ago.'

'Can't you see,' asked Doc, 'what it would do to the human race?'

'Sure. It'll make them honourable and honest. No one will ever cheat or steal again and it will be cosy . . .'

'They'll die of complicated boredom,' said Doc. 'Life will become a sort of cross between a Boy Scout jamboree and a ladies' sewing circle. There'll be no loud and unseemly argument and they'll be polite and proper to the point of stupefaction.'

'So you have changed your mind.'

'Not really, Captain. But this is the wrong way to go about it. Whatever progress the race has ever made has been achieved by the due process of social evolution. In any human advance, the villains and the rascals are as important as the forward-looking idealist. They are Man's consciences and Man can't get along without them.'

'If I were you, Doc,' I said, 'I wouldn't worry so much about the human race. It's a pretty big thing and it can take a lot of bumps. Even an overdose of honesty won't hurt it permanently.'

Actually, I didn't give a damn. I had other things on my mind right then.

Doc crossed the room and sat down on the bunk beside me. He leaned over and tapped the papers I still held in my hand.

'You got it all doped out,' he said.

I nodded bleakly. 'Yeah.'

'I thought you would.'

I shot a quick glance at him. 'You were way ahead of me. That's why you switched over.'

Doc shook his head emphatically. 'No. Please believe me, Captain, I feel as bad as you do.'

'It won't work either way.' I shuffled the papers. 'They acted in good faith. They didn't sign aboard, sure. But there was no reason that they should have. It was all understood. Share and share alike. And that's the way it's been for too long to repudiate it now. And we can't keep on. Even if we agreed to dump the stuff right here and blast off and never think of it again, we'd not get rid of it. It would always be there. The past is dead, Doc. It's spoiled. It's smashed and it can't be put back together.'

I felt like bawling. It had been a long time since I had felt that full of grief.

'They are different kind of men now,' I said. 'They went and changed themselves and they'll never be the same. Even if they could change back, it wouldn't be the same.'

Doc mocked me a little. 'The race will build a monument to you. Maybe actually on Earth itself, with all the other famous humans, for bringing back this stuff. They'd be just blind enough to do it.'

I got up and paced the floor. 'I don't want any monument. I'm not bringing it in. I'm not having anything more to do with it.'

I stood there, wishing we had never found the silo, for what had it done for me except to lose me the best crew and the best friends a man had ever had?

'The ship is mine,' I said. 'That is all I want. I'll take the cargo to the nearest point and dump it there. Hutch and the rest of

79

them can carry on from there, any way they can. They can have the honesty and honour. I'll get another crew.'

Maybe, I thought, some day it would be almost the way it had been. Almost, but not quite.

'We'll go on hunting,' I said. 'We'll dream about the jackpot. We'll do our best to find it. We'll do anything to find it. We'll break all the laws of God or Man to find it. But you know something, Doc?'

'No, I don't,' said Doc.

'I hope we never find it. I don't want to find another. I just want to go on hunting.'

We stood there in the silence, listening to the fading echoes of those days we hunted for the jackpot.

'Captain,' said Doc, 'will you take me along?'

I nodded. What was the difference? He might just as well.

'Captain, you remember those insect mounds on Suud?'

'Of course. How could I forget them?'

'You know, I've figured out a way we might break into them. Maybe we should try it. There should be a billion . . .'

I almost clobbered him.

I'm glad now that I didn't.

Suud is where we're headed.

If Doc's plan works out, we may hit that jackpot yet!

CONTRAPTION

He found the contraption in a blackberry patch when he was hunting cows. Darkness was sifting down through the tall stand of poplar trees and he couldn't make it out too well and he couldn't spend much time to look at it because Uncle Eb had been plenty sore about his missing the two heifers and if it took too long to find them Uncle Eb more than likely would take the strap to him again and he'd had about all he could stand for one day. Already he'd had to go without his supper because he'd forgotten to go down to the spring for a bucket of cold water. And Aunt Em had been after him all day because he was so no-good at weeding the garden.

'I never saw such a trifling young'un in all my life,' she'd shrill at him and then she'd go on to say that she'd think he'd have some gratitude for the way she and Uncle Eb had taken him in and saved him from the orphanage, but no, he never felt no gratitude at all, but caused all the trouble that he could and was lazy to boot and she declared to goodness she didn't know what would become of him.

He found the two heifers down in the corner of the pasture by the grove of walnut trees and drove them home, plodding along behind them, thinking once again about running away, but knowing that he wouldn't, because he had no place to go. Although, he told himself, most any place would be better than staying here with Aunt Em and Uncle Eb, who really were not his uncle and aunt at all, but just a couple of people who had took him in.

Uncle Eb was just finishing milking when he came into the

barn, driving the two heifers before him, and Uncle Eb still was plenty sore about the way he'd missed them when he'd brought in the other cows.

'Here,' said Uncle Eb, 'you've fixed it so I had to milk my share and yours, too, and all because you didn't count the cows, the way I always tell you to so you'll be sure you got them all. Just to teach you, you can finish up by milking them there heifers.'

So Johnny got his three-legged milk stool and a pail and he milked the heifers and heifers are hard things to milk, and skittish, too, and the red one kicked and knocked Johnny into the gutter, spilling the milk he had in the pail.

Uncle Eb, seeing this, took the strap down from behind the door and let Johnny have a few to teach him to be more careful and that milk represented money and then made him finish with his milking.

They went up to the house after that, Uncle Eb grumbling all the way about kids being more trouble than they're worth, and Aunt Em met them at the door to tell Johnny to be sure he washed his feet good before he went to bed because she didn't want him getting her nice clean sheets all dirty.

'Aunt Em,' he said, 'I'm awful hungry.'

'Not a bite,' she said, grim-lipped in the lamplight of the kitchen. 'Maybe if you get a little hungry you won't go forgetting all the time.'

'Just a slice of bread,' said Johnny. 'Without no butter or nothing. Just a slice of bread.'

'Young man,' said Uncle Eb, 'you heard your aunt. Get them feet washed and up to bed.'

'And see you wash them good,' said Aunt Em.

So he washed his feet and went to bed and lying there, he remembered what he had seen in the blackberry patch and remembered, too, that he hadn't said a word about it because he hadn't had a chance to, what with Uncle Eb and Aunt Em taking on at him all the blessed time.

And he decided right then and there he wouldn't tell them what he'd found, for if he did they'd take it away from him the way they always did everything he had. And if they didn't take it away from him, they'd spoil it so there'd be no fun or satisfaction in it.

The only thing he had that was really his was the old pocket knife with the point broken off the little blade. There was nothing in the world he'd rather have than another knife to replace the one he had, but he knew better than to ask for one. Once he had, and Uncle Eb and Aunt Em had carried on for days, saying what an ungrateful, grasping thing he was and here they'd gone and taken him in off the street and he still wasn't satisfied, but wanted them to spend good money for a pocket knife. Johnny worried a good deal about them saying he'd been taken in off the street, because so far as he knew he'd never been on any street.

Lying there, in his bed, looking out the window at the stars, he got to wondering what it was he'd seen in the blackberry patch and he couldn't remember it very well because he hadn't seen it too well and there'd been no time to stop and look. But there were some funny things about it and the more he thought about it, the more he wanted to have a good look at it.

Tomorrow, he thought, I'll have a good look at it. Soon as I get a chance, tomorrow. Then he realized there'd be no chance tomorrow, for Aunt Em would have him out, right after morning chores, to weed the garden and she'd keep an eye on him and there'd be no chance to slip away.

He lay in bed and thought about it some more and it became as clear as day that if he wanted a look at it he'd have to go tonight.

He could tell, by their snoring, that Uncle Eb and Aunt Em were asleep, so he got out of bed and slipped into his shirt and britches and sneaked down the stairs, being careful to miss the squeaky boards. In the kitchen he climbed up on a chair to reach the box of matches atop the warming oven of the old wood-burning stove. He took a fistful of matches, then reconsidered and put back all but half a dozen because he was afraid Aunt Em would notice if he took too many.

Outside, the grass was wet and cold with dew and he rolled up his britches so the cuffs wouldn't get all soaked, and set off across the pasture.

Going through the woods there were some spooky places, but he wasn't scared too badly, although no one could go through the woods at night without being scared a little.

Finally he got to the blackberry patch and stood there wondering how he could get through the patch in the dark without ripping his clothes and getting his bare feet full of thorns. And, standing there, he wondered if what he'd seen was still there and all at once he knew it was, for he felt a friendliness come from it, as if it might be telling him that it still was there and not to be afraid.

He was just a little unnerved, for he was not used to friendliness. The only friend he had was Benny Smith, who was about his age, and he only saw Benny during school and then not all the time, for Benny was sick a lot and had to stay home for days on end. And since Benny lived way over on the other side of the school district, he never saw him during vacation time at all.

By now his eyes were getting a little used to the darkness of the blackberry patch and he thought that he could see the darker outline of the thing that lay in there and he tried to understand how it could *feel* friendly, for he was pretty sure that it was just a thing, like a waggon or a silo-filler, and nothing alive at all. If he'd thought that it was alive, he'd been really scared.

The thing kept right on feeling friendly toward him.

So he put out his hands and tried to push the bushes apart so he could squeeze in and see what it was. If he could get close to it, he thought, he could strike the matches in his pocket and get a better look at it.

'Stop,' said the friendliness and at the word he stopped, although he wasn't sure at all that he had heard the word.

'Don't look too closely at us,' said the friendliness, and Johnny was just a little flustered at that, for he hadn't been looking at anything at all — not too closely, that is.

'All right,' he said. 'I won't look at you.' And he wondered if it was some sort of a game, like hide-and-seek that he played at school.

'After we get to be good friends,' said the thing to Johnny, 'we can look at one another and it won't matter then, for we'll know what one another is like inside and not pay attention to how we look outside.'

And Johnny, standing there, thought how they must look awful, not to want him to see them, and the thing said to him, 'We would look awful to you. You look awful to us.'

'Maybe, then,' said Johnny, 'it's a good thing I can't see in the dark.'

'You can't see in the dark?' it asked and Johnny said he

84

couldn't and there was silence for a while, although Johnny could hear it puzzling over how come he couldn't see when it was dark.

Then it asked if he could do something else and he couldn't even understand what it tried to say and finally it seemed to figure out that he couldn't do whatever it had asked about.

'You are afraid,' said the thing. 'There is no need to fear us.'

And Johnny explained that he wasn't afraid of them, whatever they might be, because they were friendly, but that he was afraid of what might happen if Uncle Eb and Aunt Em should find he had sneaked out. So they asked him a lot about Uncle Eb and Aunt Em and he tried to explain, but they didn't seem to understand, but seemed to think he was talking about government. He tried to explain how it really was, but he was pretty sure they didn't understand at all.

Finally, being polite about it so he wouldn't hurt their feelings, he said he had to leave and since he'd stayed much longer than he'd planned, he ran all the way home.

He got into the house and up to bed all right and everything was fine, but the next morning Aunt Em found the matches in his pockets and gave him a lecture about the danger of burning down the barn. To reinforce the lecture, she used a switch on his legs and try as hard as he could to be a man about it, he laid it on so hard that he jumped up and down and screamed.

He worked through the day weeding the garden and just before dark went to get the cows.

He didn't have to go out of his way to go past the blackberry patch, for the cows were in that direction, but he knew well enough that if they hadn't been, he'd gone out of his way, for he'd been remembering all day the friendliness he'd found there.

It was still daylight this time, just shading into night, and he could see that the thing, whatever it might be, was not alive, but simply a hunk of metal, like two sauce dishes stuck together, with a rim running around its middle just like there'd be a rim if you stuck two dishes together. It looked like old metal that had been laying around for a long time and you could see where it was pitted like a piece of machinery will get when it stands out in the weather.

It had crushed a path for quite a ways through the blackberry thicket and had ploughed up the ground for twenty feet or so, and, sighting back along the way it had come, Johnny could see where it had hit and smashed the top of a tall poplar.

It spoke to him, without words, the way it had the night before, with friendliness and fellowship, although Johnny wouldn't know that last word, never having run across it in his school books.

It said, 'You may look at us a little now. Look at us quick and then away. Don't look at us steadily. Just a quick look and then away. That way you get used to us. A little at a time.'

'Where are you?' Johnny asked.

'Right here,' they said.

'Inside of there?' asked Johnny.

'Inside of here,' they said.

'I can't see you, then,' said Johnny. 'I can't see through metal.'

'He can't see through metal,' said one of them.

'He can't see when the star is gone,' said the other.

'He can't see us, then,' they said, the both of them.

'You might come out,' said Johnny.

'We can't come out,' they said. 'We'd die if we came out.'

'I can't ever see you, then.'

'You can't ever see us, Johnny.'

And he stood there, feeling terribly lonely because he could never see these friends of his.

'We don't understand who you are,' they said. 'Tell us who you are.'

And because they were so kind and friendly, he told them who he was and how he was an orphan and had been taken in by his Uncle Eb and Aunt Em, who really weren't his aunt and uncle. He didn't tell them how Uncle Eb and Aunt Em treated him, whipping him and scolding him and sending him to bed without his supper, but this, too, as well as the things he told them, was there for them to sense and now there was more than friendliness, more than fellowship. Now there was compassion and something that was their equivalent of mother love.

'He's just a little one,' they said, talking to one another.

They reached out to him and seemed to take him in their arms and hold him tight against them and Johnny went down on his knees without knowing it and held out his arms to the thing that lay there among the broken bushes and cried out to

86

them, as if there was something there that he might grasp and hold – some comfort that he had always missed and longed for and now finally had found. His heart cried out the thing that he could not say, the pleading that would not pass his lips, and they answered him.

'No, we'll not leave you, Johnny. We can't leave you, Johnny.'

'You promise?' Johnny asked.

Their voice was a little grim. 'We do not need to promise, Johnny. Our machine is broken and we cannot fix it. One of us is dying and the other will soon die.'

Johnny knelt there, with the words sinking into him, with the realization sinking into him, and it seemed more than he could bear that, having found two friends, they were about to die.

'Johnny,' they said to him.

'Yes,' said Johnny, trying not to cry.

'You will trade with us?'

'Trade?'

'A way of friendship with us. You give us something and we give you something.'

'But,' said Johnny. 'But I haven't . . .'

Then he knew he had. He had the pocket knife. It wasn't much, with its broken blade, but it was all he had.

'That is fine,' they said. 'That is exactly right. Lay it on the ground, close to the machine.'

He took the knife out of his pocket and laid it against the machine and even as he watched something happened, but it happened so fast he couldn't see how it worked, but, anyhow, the knife was gone and there was something in its place.

'Thank you, Johnny,' they said. 'It was nice of you to trade with us.'

He reached out his hand and took the thing they'd traded him and even in the darkness it flashed with hidden fire. He turned it in the palm of his hand and saw that it was some sort of jewel, many-faceted, and that the glow came from inside of it and that it burned with many different colours.

It wasn't until he saw how much light came from it that he realized how long he'd stayed and how dark it was and when he saw that he jumped to his feet and ran, without waiting to say goodbye.

It was too dark now to look for the cows and he hoped they had started home alone and that he could catch up with them and bring them in. He'd tell Uncle Eb that he'd had a hard time rounding them up. He'd tell Uncle Eb that the two heifers had broken out of the fence and he had to get them back. He'd tell Uncle Eb . . . he'd tell . . . he'd tell . . .

His breath gasped with his running and his heart was thumping so it seemed to shake him and fear rode on his shoulders — fear of the awful thing he'd done — of this final unforgivable thing after all the others, after not going to the spring to get the water, after missing the two heifers the night before, after the matches in his pocket.

He did not find the cows going home alone — he found them in the barnyard and he knew that they'd been milked and he knew he'd stayed much longer and that it was far worse than he had imagined.

He walked up the rise to the house, shaking now with fear. There was a light in the kitchen and he knew that they were waiting.

He came into the kitchen and they sat at the table, facing him, waiting for him, with the lamplight on their faces and their faces were so hard that they looked like graven stone.

Uncle Eb stood up, towering toward the ceiling, and you could see the muscles stand out on his arms, with the sleeves rolled to the elbow.

He reached for Johnny and Johnny ducked away, but the hand closed on the back of his neck and the fingers wrapped around his throat and lifted him and shook him with a silent savagery.

'I'll teach you,' Uncle Eb was saying through clenched teeth. 'I'll teach you. I'll teach you . . .'

Something fell upon the floor and rolled toward the corner, leaving a trail of fire as it rolled along the floor.

Uncle Eb stopped shaking him and just stood there holding him for an instant, then dropped him to the floor.

'That fell out of your pocket,' said Uncle Eb. 'What is it?'

Johnny backed away, shaking his head.

He wouldn't tell what it was. He'd never tell. No matter what Uncle Eb might do to him, he'd never tell. Not even if he killed him.

Uncle Eb stalked the jewel, bent swiftly and picked it up. He

88

carried it back to the table and dropped it there and bent over, looking at it, sparkling in the light.

Aunt Em leaned forward in her chair to look at it.

'What in the world!' she said.

They bent there for a moment, staring at the jewel, their eyes bright and shining, their bodies tense, their breath rasping in the silence. The world could have come to an end right then and there and they'd never noticed.

Then they straightened up and turned to look at Johnny, turning away from the jewel as if it didn't interest them any longer, as if it had had a job to do and had done that job and no longer was important. There was something wrong with them – no, not wrong, but different.

'You must be starved,' Aunt Em said to Johnny. 'I'll warm you up some supper. Would you like some eggs?'

Johnny gulped and nodded.

Uncle Eb sat down, not paying any attention to the jewel at all.

'You know,' he said, 'I saw a jackknife uptown the other day. Just the kind you want . . .'

Johnny scarcely heard him.

He just stood there, listening to the friendliness and love that hummed through all the house.

COURTESY

The serum was no good. The labels told the story.

Dr James H. Morgan took his glasses off and wiped them carefully, cold terror clutching at his innards. He put the spectacles back on, probing at them with a thick, blunt finger to settle them into correct position. Then he took another look. He had been right the first time. The date on the serum consignment was a good ten years too old.

He wheeled slowly, lumbered a few ponderous steps to the tent flap and stood there, squat body framed in the triangular entrance, pudgy hands gripping the canvas on either side.

Outside, the fantastic lichen moors stretched to grey and bleak horizons. The setting sun was a dull red glow in the west – and to the east, the doctor knew, night already was beginning to close in, with that veil of purplish light that seemed to fall like a curtain upon the land and billow rapidly across it.

A chill wind blew out of the east, already touched with the frigidity of night, and twitched the canvas beneath the doctor's fingers.

'Ah, yes,' said Dr Morgan, 'the merry moors of Landro.'

A lonely place, he told himself. Not lonely only in its barrenness nor in its alien wildness, but with an ingrained loneliness that could drive a man mad if he were left alone with it.

Like a great cemetery, he thought, an empty place of dead. And yet without the cemetery's close association, without the tenderness and the inevitability of a cemetery. For a cemetery held in sacred trust the husks of those who once had lived and this place was an emptiness that held no memory at all.

But not for long, said Dr Morgan. Not for long now.

He stood looking at the barren slope that rose above the camp and he decided that it would make an eminently satisfactory cemetery.

All places looked alike. That was the trouble. You couldn't tell one place from another. There were no trees and there were no bushes, just a fuzzy-looking scrub that grew here and there, clothing the naked land in splotches, like the ragged coat that a beggar wears.

Benny Falkner stopped on the path as it topped the rise and stood rigid with the fear that was mounting in him. Fear of the coming night and of its bitter cold, fear of the silent hills and the shadowed swales, and the more distant and yet more terrible fear of the little natives that might this very moment be skulking on the hillside.

He put up his arm and wiped the sweat off his brow with his tattered sleeve. He shouldn't have been sweating, he told himself, for it was chilly now and getting colder by the minute. In another hour or two it would be cold enough to freeze a man unprotected in the open.

He fought down the terror that choked his throat and set his teeth a-chatter and for an instant stood stock-still to convince himself he was not panic-stricken.

He had been going east and that meant he must go west to reach the camp again. Although the catch was that he couldn't be absolutely sure he had been going east all the time – he might have trended north a little or even wandered south. But the deviation couldn't have been enough, he was sure, to throw him so far off that he could not spot the camp by returning straight into the west.

Sometime soon he should sight the smoke of the Earthmen's camp. Any ridge, the next ridge, each succeeding hummock in the winding trail, he had assured himself, would bring him upon the camp itself. He would reach higher ground and there the camp would be, spread out in front of him, with the semicircle of white canvas gleaming in the fading light and the thin trail of smoke rising from the larger cook tent where Bat Ears Brady would be bellowing one of his obscene songs.

But that had been an hour ago when the sun still stood a good two hands high. He remembered now, standing on the ridge-top, that he had been a little nervous, but not really apprehensive. It had been unthinkable, then, that a man could get himself lost in an hour's walk out of camp.

Now the sun was gone and the cold was creeping in and the wind had a lonely sound he had not noticed when the light was good.

One more rise, he decided. One more ridge, and if that is not the one, I'll give up until morning. Find a sheltered place somewhere, a rock face of some sort that will give me some protection and reflect a campfire's heat — if I can find anything with which to make a campfire.

He stood and listened to the wind moaning across the land behind him and it seemed to him there was a whimper in the sound, as if the wind were anxious, that it might be following on his track, sniffing out his scent.

Then he heard the other sound, the soft, padding sound that came up the hill toward him.

Ira Warren sat at his desk and stared accusingly at the paper work stacked in front of him. Reluctantly he took some of the papers off the stack and laid them on the desk.

That fool Falkner, he thought. I've told them and I've told them that they have to stick together, that no one must go wandering off alone.

A bunch of babies, he told himself savagely. Just a bunch of drooling kids, fresh out of college, barely dry behind the ears and all hopped up with erudition, but without any common sense. And not a one of them would listen. That was the worst of it, not a one of them would listen.

Someone scratched on the canvas of the tent.

'Come in,' called Warren.

Dr Morgan entered.

'Good evening, commander,' he said.

'Well,' said Warren irritably, 'what now?'

'Why, now,' said Dr Morgan, sweating just a little. 'It's the matter of the serum.'

'The serum?'

'The serum,' said Dr Morgan. 'It isn't any good.'

'What do you mean?' asked Warren. 'I have troubles, doctor. I can't play patty-cake with you about your serum.'

'It's too old,' said Morgan. 'A good ten years too old. You can't use old serum. You see, it might . . .'

'Stop chattering,' commanded Warren, sharply. 'The serum is too old, you say. When did you find this out?'

'Just now.'

'You mean this very moment?'

Morgan nodded miserably.

Warren pushed the papers to one side very carefully and deliberately. He placed his hands on the desk in front of him and made a tent out of his fingers.

'Tell me this, doctor,' said Warren, speaking cautiously, as if he were hunting in his mind for the exact words which he must use, 'how long has this expedition been on Landro?'

'Why,' said Morgan, 'quite some time, I'd say.' He counted mental fingers. 'Six weeks, to be exact.'

'And the serum has been here all that time?'

'Why, of course,' said Morgan. 'It was unloaded from the ship at the same time as all the other stuff.'

'It wasn't left around somewhere, so that you just found it? It was taken to your tent at once?'

'Of course it was,' said Morgan. 'The very first thing. I always insist upon that procedure.'

'At any time in the last six weeks, at any given moment in any day of that whole six weeks, you could have inspected the serum and found it was no good? Isn't that correct, doctor?'

'I suppose I could have,' Morgan admitted. 'It was just that . . .'

'You didn't have the time,' suggested Warren, sweetly.

'Well, not that,' said Morgan.

'You were, perhaps, too pressed with other interests?'

'Well, not exactly.'

'You were aware that up to a week ago we could have contacted the ship by radio and it could have turned back and took us off. They would have done that if we had let them know about the serum.'

'I know that.'

'And you know now that they're outside our radio range. We can't let them know. We can't call them back. We won't have any contact with the human race for the next two years.'

'I,' said Morgan, weakly, 'I . . .'

'It's been lovely knowing you,' Warren told him. 'Just how long do you figure it will be before we are dead?'

'It will be another week or so before we'll become susceptible to the virus,' Morgan said. 'It will take, in certain stubborn cases, six weeks or so for it to kill a man.'

'Two months,' said Warren. 'Three, at the outside. Would you say that was right, Dr Morgan?'

'Yes,' said Morgan.

'There is something that I want you to tell me,' Warren said.

'What is it?' Morgan asked.

'Sometime when you have a moment, when you have the time and it is no inconvenience to you, I should like to know just how it feels to kill twenty-five of your fellow men.'

'I,' said Morgan, 'I . . .'

'And yourself, of course,' said Warren. 'That makes twenty-six.'

Bat Ears Brady was a character. For more than thirty years now he had been going out on planetary expeditions with Commander Ira Warren, although Warren had not been a commander when it started, but a second looey. Today they were still together, a team of toughened planet-checkers. Although no one on the outside would have known that they were a team, for Warren headed the expeditions and Bat Ears cooked for them.

Now Warren set out a bottle on his desk and sent for Bat Ears Brady.

Warren heard him coming for some time before he finally arrived. He'd had a drink or two too many and he was singing most obscenely.

He came through the tent entrance walking stiff and straight, as if there were a chalked line laid out for him to follow. He saw the bottle on the desk and picked it up, disregarding the glasses set beside it. He lowered the bottle by a good three inches and set it back again. Then he took the camp chair that had been placed there for him.

'What's the matter now?' he demanded. 'You never send for me unless there's something wrong.'

'What,' asked Warren, 'have you been drinking?'

Bat Ears hiccuped politely. 'Little something I cooked up.'

He regarded Warren balefully. 'Use to be we could bring in a little something, but now they say we can't. What little there is you keep under lock and key. When a man gets thirsty, it sure tests his ingen . . . ingen . . . ingen . . .'

'Ingenuity,' said Warren.

'That's the word,' said Bat Ears. 'That's the word, exactly.'

'We're in a jam, Bat Ears,' said Warren.

'We're always in a jam,' said Bat Ears. 'Ain't like the old days, Ira. Had some he-men then. But now . . .'

'I know what you mean,' said Warren.

'Kids,' said Bat Ears, spitting on the floor in a gesture of contempt. 'Scarcely out of didies. Got to wipe their noses and . . .'

'It isn't that kind of a jam,' said Warren. 'This is the real McCoy. If we can't figure this one out, we'll all be dead before two months are gone.'

'Natives?' asked Bat Ears.

'Not the natives,' Warren told him. 'Although more than likely they'd be glad to do us in if there was a chance.'

'Cheeky customers,' said Bat Ears. 'One of them sneaked into the cook tent and I kicked him off the reservation real unceremonious. He did considerable squalling at me. He didn't like it none.'

'You shouldn't kick them, Bat Ears.'

'Well, Ira, I didn't really kick him. That was just a figure of speech, kind of. No sir, I didn't kick him. I took a shovel to him. Always could handle a shovel some better than my feet. Reach farther and . . .'

He reached out and took the bottle, lowered it another inch or two.

'This crisis, Ira?'

'It's the serum,' Warren told him. 'Morgan waited until the ship had got too far for us to contact them before he thought to check the serum. And it isn't any good – it's about ten years too old.'

Bat Ears sat half stunned.

'So we don't get our booster shots,' said Warren, 'and that means that we will die. There's this deadly virus here, the . . . the – oh, well, I can't remember the name of it. But you know about it.'

'Sure,' said Bat Ears. 'Sure I know about it.'

'Funny thing,' said Warren. 'You'd expect to find something like that on one of the jungle planets. But, no, you find it here. Something about the natives. They're humanoid. Got the same kind of guts we got. So the virus developed an ability to attack a humanoid system. We are good, new material for it.'

'It don't seem to bother the natives none now,' said Bat Ears.

'No,' said Warren. 'They seem to be immune. One of two things: They've found a cure or they've developed natural immunity.'

'If they've found a cure,' said Bat Ears, 'we can shake it out of them.'

'And if they haven't,' said Warren, 'if adaptation is the answer – then we're dead ducks for sure.'

'We'll start working on them,' said Bat Ears. 'They hate us and they'd love to see us croak, but we'll find some way to get it out of them.'

'Everything always hates us,' Warren said. 'Why is that, Bat Ears? We do our best and they always hate us. On every planet that Man has set a foot on. We try to make them like us, we do all we can for them. But they resent our help. Or reject our friendliness. Or take us for a bunch of suckers – so that finally we lose our patience and we take a shovel to them.'

'And then,' said Bat Ears, sanctimoniously, 'the fat is in the fire.'

'What I'm worried about is the men,' said Warren. 'When they hear about this serum business . . .'

'We can't tell them,' said Bat Ears. 'We can't let them know. They'll find out, after a while, of course, but not right away.'

'Morgan is the only one who knows,' said Warren, 'and he blabs. We can't keep him quiet. It'll be all over camp by morning.'

Bat Ears rose ponderously. He towered over Warren as he reached out a hand for the bottle on the desk.

'I'll drop in on Morgan on my way back,' he said. 'I'll fix it so he won't talk.'

He took a long pull at the bottle and set it back.

'I'll draw a picture of what'll happen to him if he does,' said Bat Ears.

Warren sat easily in his chair, watching the retreating back of Bat Ears Brady. Always there in a pinch, he thought. Always a man that you can depend on.

Bat Ears was back in three minutes flat. He stood in the entrance of the tent, no sign of drunkenness upon him, his face solemn, eyes large with the thing he'd seen.

'He croaked himself,' he said.

That was the solemn truth.

Dr James H. Morgan lay dead inside his tent, his throat sliced open with a professional nicety that no one but a surgeon could have managed.

About midnight the searching party brought in Falkner.

Warren stared wearily at him. The kid was scared. He was all scratched up from floundering around in the darkness and he was pale around the gills.

'He saw our light, sir,' said Peabody, 'and let out a yell. That's the way we found him.'

'Thank you, Peabody,' said Warren. 'I'll see you in the morning. I want to talk to Falkner.'

'Yes, sir,' said Peabody. 'I am glad we found him, sir.'

Wish I had more like him, thought Warren. Bat Ears, the ancient planet-checker; Peabody, an old army man, and Gilmer, the grizzled supply officer. Those are the ones to count on. The rest of them are punks.

Falkner tried to stand stiff and straight.

'You see, sir,' he told Warren, 'it was like this: I thought I saw an outcropping . . .'

Warren interrupted him. 'You know, of course, Mr Falkner, that it is an expedition rule you never are to go out by yourself; that under no circumstance is one to go off by himself.'

'Yes, sir,' said Falkner, 'I know that . . .'

'You are aware,' said Warren, 'that you are alive only by some incredible quirk of fate. You would have frozen before morning if the natives hadn't got you first.'

'I saw a native, sir. He didn't bother me.'

'You are more than lucky, then,' said Warren. 'It isn't often that a native hasn't got the time to spare to slit a human's throat. In the five expeditions that have been here before us, they have killed a full eighteen. Those stone knives they have, I can assure you, make very ragged slitting.'

Warren drew a record book in front of him, opened it and made a very careful notation.

'Mr Falkner,' he said, 'you will be confined to camp for a

two-week period for infraction of the rules. Also, during that time, you shall be attached to Mr Brady.'

'Mr Brady, sir? The cook?'

'Precisely,' said Warren. 'He probably shall want you to hustle fuel and help with the meals and dispose of garbage and other such light tasks.'

'But I was sent on this expedition to make geologic observations, not to help the cook.'

'All very true,' admitted Warren. 'But, likewise, you were sent out under certain regulations. You have seen fit to disregard those regulations and I see fit, as a result, to discipline you. That is all, Mr Falkner.'

Falkner turned stiffly and moved toward the tent flap.

'By the way,' said Warren, 'I forgot to tell you. I'm glad that you got back.'

Falkner did not answer.

Warren stiffened for a moment, then relaxed. After all, he thought, what did it matter? Within another few weeks nothing would matter for him and Falkner, nor for any of the rest.

The chaplain showed up the first thing in the morning. Warren was sitting on the edge of his cot, pulling on his trousers when the man came in. It was cold and Warren was shivering despite the sputtering of the little stove that stood beside the desk.

The chaplain was very precise and businesslike about his visit.

'I thought I should talk with you,' he said, 'about arranging services for our dear departed friend.'

'What dear departed friend?' asked Warren, shivering and pulling on a shoe.

'Why, Dr Morgan, of course.'

'I see,' said Warren. 'Yes, I suppose we shall have to bury him.'

The chaplain stiffened just a little.

'I was wondering if the doctor had any religious convictions, any sort of preference.'

'I doubt it very much,' said Warren. 'If I were you, I'd hold it down to minimum simplicity.'

'That's what I thought,' said the chaplain. 'A few words, perhaps, and a simple prayer.'

'Yes,' said Warren. 'A prayer by all means. We'll need a lot of prayer.'

'Pardon me, sir?'

'Oh,' Warren told him, 'don't mind me. Just wool-gathering, that's all.'

'I see,' said the chaplain. 'I was wondering, sir, if you have any idea what might have made him do it.'

'Who do what?'

'What made the doctor commit suicide.'

'Oh, that,' said Warren. 'Just an unstable character, I guess.'

He laced his shoes and stood up.

'Mr Barnes,' he said, 'you are a man of God, and a very good one from what I've seen of you. You may have the answer to a question that is bothering me.'

'Why,' said Mr Barnes, 'why I . . .'

'What would you do,' asked Warren, 'if you suddenly were to find you had no more than two months to live?'

'Why,' said Mr Barnes, 'I suppose that I would go on living pretty much the way I always have. With a little closer attention to the condition of my soul, perhaps.'

'That,' said Warren, 'is a practical answer. And, I suppose, the most reasonable that anyone can give.'

The chaplain looked at him curiously. 'You don't mean, sir . . .'

'Sit down, Barnes,' said Warren. 'I'll turn up the stove. I need you now. To tell you the solemn truth, I've never held too much with this business of having you fellows with the expedition. But I guess there always will be times when one needs a man like you.'

The chaplain sat down.

'Mr Barnes,' said Warren, 'that was no hypothetical question I asked. Unless God performs some miracle we'll all be dead in another two months' time.'

'You are joking, sir.'

'Not at all,' said Warren. 'The serum is no good. Morgan waited to check it until it was too late to get word to the ship. That's why he killed himself.'

He watched the chaplain closely and the chaplain did not flinch.

'I was of a mind,' said Warren, 'not to tell you. I'm not telling any of the others – not for a while, at least.'

'It takes a little while,' said Mr Barnes, 'to let a thing like that soak in. I find it so, myself. Maybe you should tell the others, let them have a chance . . .'

'No,' said Warren.

The chaplain stared at him. 'What are you hoping for, Warren? What do you expect to happen?'

'A miracle,' said Warren.

'A miracle?'

'Certainly,' said Warren. 'You believe in miracles. You must.'

'I don't know,' said Mr Barnes. 'There are certain miracles, of course — one might call them allegorical miracles, and sometimes men read into them more than was ever meant.'

'I am more practical than that,' said Warren, harshly. 'There is the miracle of the fact that the natives of this place are humanoid like ourselves and they don't need any booster shots. There is a potential miracle in the fact that only the first humans who landed on the planet ever tried to live on Landro without the aid of booster shots.'

'Since you mention it,' said the chaplain, 'there is the miracle of the fact that we are here at all.'

Warren blinked at him. 'That's right,' he said. 'Tell me, why do you think we're here? Divine destiny, perhaps. Or the immutable performance of the mysterious forces that move Man along his way.'

'We are here,' said Barnes, 'to carry on the survey work that has been continued thus far by parties here before us.'

'And that will be continued,' said Warren, 'by the parties that come after us.'

'You forget,' the chaplain said, 'that all of us will die. They will be very wary of sending another expedition to replace one that has been wiped out.'

'And you,' said Warren, 'forget the miracle.'

The report had been written by the psychologist who had accompanied the third expedition to Landro. Warren had managed, after considerable digging in the file of quadruplicates, to find a copy of it.

'Hog wash,' he said and struck the papers with his fist.

'I could of told you that,' said Bat Ears, 'before you ever read it. Ain't nothing one of them prissy punks can tell an old-timer like me about these abor . . . abor . . . abor . . .'

'Aborigines,' said Warren.

'That's the word,' said Bat Ears. 'That's the word I wanted.'

'It says here,' declared Warren, 'that the natives of Landro have a keen sense of dignity, very delicately tuned – that's the very words it uses – and an exact code of honour when dealing among themselves.'

Bat Ears snorted and reached for the bottle. He took a drink and sloshed what was left in the bottom discontentedly.

'You sure,' he asked, 'that this is all you got?'

'You should know,' snapped Warren.

Bat Ears wagged his head. 'Comforting thing,' he said. 'Mighty comforting.'

'It says,' went on Warren, 'that they also have a system of what amounts to protocol, on a rather primitive basis.'

'I don't know about this proto-whatever-you-may-call-it,' said Bat Ears, 'but that part about the code of honour gets me. Why, them dirty vultures would steal the pennies off a dead man's eyes. I always keep a shovel handy and when one of them shows up . . .'

'The report,' said Warren, 'goes into that most exhaustively. Explains it.'

'Ain't no need of explanation,' insisted Bat Ears. 'They just want what you got, so they sneak in and take it.'

'Says it's like stealing from a rich man,' Warren told him. 'Like a kid that sees a field with a million melons in it. Kid can't see anything wrong with taking one melon out of all that million.'

'We ain't got no million melons,' said Bat Ears.

'It's just an analogy,' said Warren. 'The stuff we have here must look like a million melons to our little friends.'

'Just the same,' protested Bat Ears, 'they better keep out of my cook tent . . .'

'Shut up,' said Warren savagely. 'I get you here to talk with you and all you do is drink up my liquor and caterwaul about your cook tent.'

'All right,' said Bat Ears. 'All right. What do you want to know?'

'What are we doing about contacting the natives?'

'Can't contact them,' said Bat Ears, 'if we can't find them. They were around here, thicker than fleas, before we needed them. Now that we need them, can't find hide nor hair of one.'

'As if they might know that we needed them,' said Warren.

'How would they know?' asked Bat Ears.

'I can't tell you,' Warren said. 'It was just a thought.'

'If you do find them,' asked Bat Ears, 'how you going to make them talk?'

'Bribe them,' said Warren. 'Buy them. Offer them anything we have.'

Bat Ears shook his head. 'It won't work. Because they know all they got to do is wait. If they just wait long enough, it's theirs without the asking. I got a better way.'

'Your way won't work, either.'

'You're wasting your time, anyhow,' Bat Ears told him. 'They ain't got no cure. It's just adap . . . adap . . .'

'Adaptation.'

'Sure,' said Bat Ears. 'That's the word I meant.'

He took up the bottle, shook it, measured it with his thumb and then, in a sudden gesture, killed it.

He rose quickly to his feet. 'I got to sling some grub together,' he said. 'You stay here and get her figured out.'

Warren sat quietly in the tent, listening to his footsteps going across the compound of the camp.

There was no hope, of course. He must have known that all along, he told himself, and yet he had postponed the realization of it. Postponed it with talk of miracles and hope that the natives might have the answer – and the native answer, the native cure, he admitted now, was even more fantastic than the hope of a miracle. For how could one expect the little owl-eyed people would know of medicine when they did not know of clothing, when they still carried rudely-chipped stone knives, when their campfire was a thing very laboriously arrived at by the use of stricken flint?

They would die, all twenty-five of them, and in the days to come the little owl-eyed natives would come boldly marching in, no longer skulking, and pick the camp to its last bare bone.

Collins was the first to go. He died hard, as all men die hard when infected by the peculiar virus of Landro. Before he was dead, Peabody had taken to his bed with the dull headache that heralded the onset of the malady. After that the men went down like ten pins. They screamed and moaned in delirium, they lay as dead for days before they finally died, while the fever ate at them like some ravenous animal that had crept in from the moors.

There was little that anyone could do. Make them comfortble, keep them bathed and the bedding washed and changed, feed them broth that Bat Ears made in big kettles on the stove, be sure there was fresh, cold water always available for the fever-anguished throats.

At first the graves were deep and wooden crosses were set up, with the name and other information painted on the cross bar. Then the graves were only shallow holes because there were less hands to dig them and less strength within the hands.

To Warren it was a nightmare of eternity – a ceaseless round of caring for his stricken men, of helping with the graves, of writing in the record book the names of those who died. Sleep came in snatches when he could catch it or when he became so exhausted that he tottered in his tracks and could not keep his eyelids open. Food was something that Bat Ears brought and set in front of him and he gulped without knowing what it was, without tasting what it was.

Time was a forgotten thing and he lost track of days. He asked what day it was and no one knew nor seemed to care. The sun came up and the sun went down and the moors stretched to their grey horizons, with the lonely wind blowing out of them.

Vaguely he became aware of fewer and fewer men who worked beside him, of fewer stricken men upon the cots. And one day he sat down in his tent and looked across at another haggard face and knew it was nearly over.

'It's a cruel thing, sir,' said the haggard face.

'Yes, Mr Barnes,' said Warren. 'How many are there left?'

'Three,' said the chaplain, 'and two of them are nearly gone. Young Falkner seems to be better, though.'

'Any on their feet?'

'Bat Ears, sir. Just you and I and Bat Ears.'

'Why don't we catch it, Barnes? Why are we still here?'

'No one knows,' the chaplain told him. 'I have a feeling that we'll not escape it.'

'I know,' said Warren. 'I have that feeling, too.'

Bat Ears lumbered into the tent and set a pail upon the table. He reached into it and scooped out a tin cup, dripping, and handed it to Warren.

'What is it, Bat Ears?' Warren asked.

'Something I cooked up,' said Bat Ears. 'Something that you need.'

Warren lifted the cup and gulped it down. It burned its way clear into his stomach, set his throat afire and exploded in his head.

'Potatoes,' said Bat Ears. 'Spuds make powerful stuff. The Irish found that out, years and years ago.'

He took the cup from Warren, dipped it again and handed it to Barnes.

The chaplain hesitated.

Bat Ears shouted at him. 'Drink it, man. It'll put some heart in you.'

The minister drank, choked, set the cup back on the table empty.

'They're back again,' said Bat Ears.

'Who's back?' asked Warren.

'The natives,' said Bat Ears. 'All around us, waiting for the end of us.'

He disdained the cup, lifted the pail in both his hands and put it to his lips. Some of the liquor splashed out of the corners of his mouth and ran darkly down his shirt.

He put the pail back on the table, wiped his mouth with a hairy fist.

'They might at least be decent about it,' he declared. 'They might at least keep out of sight until it is all over. Caught one sneaking out of Falkner's tent. Old grey buck. Tried to catch him, but he outlegged me.'

'Falkner's tent?'

'Sure. Snooping around before a man is dead. Not even waiting till he's gone. Didn't take nothing, though, I guess. Falkner was asleep. Didn't even wake him.'

'Asleep? You sure?'

'Sure,' said Bat Ears. 'Breathing natural. I'm going to unsling my gun and pick off a few of them, just for luck. I'll teach them . . .'

'Mr Brady,' asked Barnes, 'you are certain Falkner was sleeping naturally? Not in a coma? Not dead?'

'I know when a man is dead,' yelled Bat Ears.

*

104

Jones and Webster died during the night. Warren found Bat Ears in the morning, collapsed beside his stone-cold stove, the empty liquor pail beside him. At first he thought the cook was only drunk and then he saw the signs upon him. He hauled him across the floor and boosted him onto his cot, then went out to find the chaplain.

He found him in the cemetery, wielding a shovel, his hands red with broken blisters.

'It won't be deep,' said Mr Barnes, 'but it will cover them. It's the best that I can do.'

'Bat Ears has it,' Warren told him.

The chaplain leaned on his shovel, breathing a little hard from digging.

'Queer,' he said. 'Queer, to think of him. Of big, brawling Bat Ears. He was a tower of strength.

Warren reached for the shovel.

'I'll finish this,' he said, 'if you'll go down and get them ready. I can't . . . I haven't the heart to handle them.'

The chaplain handed over the shovel. 'It's funny,' he said, 'about young Falkner.'

'You said yesterday he was a little better. You imagined it?'

Barnes shook his head. 'I was in to see him. He's awake and lucid and his temperature is down.'

They stared at one another for a long time, each trying to hide the hope that might be upon his face.

'Do you think . . .'

'No, I don't,' said Barnes.

But Falkner continued to improve. Three days later he was sitting up. Six days later he stood with the other two beside the grave when they buried Bat Ears.

And there were three of them. Three out of twenty-six.

The chaplain closed his book and put it in his pocket. Warren took up the shovel and shovelled in the dirt. The other two watched him silently as he filled the grave, slowly, deliberately, taking his time, for there was no other task to hurry him – filled it and mounded it and shaped it neat and smooth with gentle shovel pats.

Then the three of them went down the slope together, not arm in arm, but close enough to have been arm in arm – back to the white tents of the camp.

Still they did not talk.

It was as if they understood for the moment the dedicatory value of the silence that lay upon the land and upon the camp and the three that were left out of twenty-six.

Falkner said: 'There is nothing strange about me. Nothing different than any other man.'

'There must be,' insisted Warren. 'You survived the virus. It hit you and you came out alive. There must be a reason for it.'

'You two,' said Falkner, 'never even got it. There must be some reason for that, too.'

'We can't be sure,' said Chaplain Barnes, speaking softly.

Warren rustled his notes angrily.

'We've covered it,' he said. 'Covered everything that you can remember – unless you are holding back something that we should know.'

'Why should I hold back anything?' demanded Falkner.

'Childhood history,' said Warren. 'The usual things. Measles, a slight attack of whooping cough, colds – afraid of the dark. Ordinary eating habits, normal acceptance of schools and social obligations. Everything as if it might be someone else. But there has to be an answer. Something that you did . . .'

'Or,' said Barnes, 'even something that he thought.'

'Huh?' asked Warren.

'The ones who could tell us are out there on the slope,' said Barnes. 'You and I, Warren, are stumbling along a path we are not equipped to travel. A medical man, a psychologist, even an alien psychologist, a statistician – any one of them would have had something to contribute. But they are dead. You and I are trying to do something we have no training for. We might have the answer right beneath our noses and we would not recognize it.'

'I know,' said Warren. 'I know. We only do the best we can.'

'I have told you everything I can,' said Falkner, tensely. 'Everything I know. I've told you things I would not tell under any other circumstance.'

'We know, lad,' said Barnes gently. 'We know you have.'

'Somewhere,' persisted Warren, 'somewhere in the life of Benjamin Falkner there is an answer – an answer to the thing that Man must know. Something that he has forgotten. Something that he has not told us, unintentionally. Or, more than likely, something that he has told us and we do not recognize.'

'Or,' said Barnes, 'something that no one but a specialist

could know. Some strange quirk in his body or his mind. Some tiny mutation that no one would suspect. Or even . . . Warren, you remember, you talked to me about a miracle.'

'I'm tired of it,' Falkner told them. 'For three days now you have gone over me, pawed me, questioned me, dissected every thought . . .'

'Let's go over that last part again,' said Warren wearily. 'When you were lost.'

'We've gone over it,' said Falkner, 'a hundred times already.'

'Once again,' said Warren. 'Just once again. You were standing there, on the path, you say, when you heard the footsteps coming up the path.'

'Not footsteps,' said Falkner. 'At first I didn't know they were footsteps. It was just a sound.'

'And it terrified you?'

'It terrified me.'

'Why?'

'Well, the dark, and being lost and . . .'

'You'd been thinking about the natives?'

'Well, yes, off and on.'

'More than off and on?'

'More than off and on,' Falkner admitted. 'All the time, maybe. Ever since I realized I was lost, perhaps. In the back of my mind.'

'Finally you realized they were footsteps?'

'No. I didn't know what they were until I saw the native.'

'Just one native?'

'Just one. An old one. His coat was all grey and he had a scar across his face. You could see the jagged white line.'

'You're sure about that scar?'

'Yes.'

'Sure about his being old?'

'He looked old. He was all grey. He walked slowly and he had a limp.'

'And you weren't afraid?'

'Yes, afraid, of course. But not as afraid as I would have expected.'

'You would have killed him if you could?'

'No, I wouldn't have killed him.'

'Not even to save your life?'

107

'Oh, sure. But I didn't think of that. I just . . . well, I just didn't want to tangle with him, that is all.'

'You got a good look at him?'

'Yes, a good look. He passed me no farther away than you are now.'

'You would recognize him again if you saw him?'

'I did recognize . . .'

Falkner stopped, befuddled.

'Just a minute,' he said. 'Just a minute now.'

He put up his hand and rubbed hard against his forehead. His eyes suddenly had a stricken look.

'I did see him again,' he said. 'I recognized him. I know it was the same one.'

Warren burst out angrily: 'Why didn't you tell . . .'

But Barnes rushed in and headed him off:

'You saw him again. When?'

'In my tent. When I was sick. I opened my eyes and he was there in front of me.'

'Just standing there?'

'Standing there and looking me. Like he was going to swallow me with those big yellow eyes of his. Then he . . . then he . . .'

They waited for him to remember.

'I was sick,' said Falkner. 'Out of my head, maybe. Not all there. I can't be sure. But it seemed that he stretched out his hands, his paws rather – that he stretched them out and touched me, one paw on each side of my head.'

'Touched you? Actually, physically touched you?'

'Gently,' said Falkner. 'Ever so gently. Just for an instant. Then I went to sleep.'

'We're ahead of our story,' Warren said impatiently. 'Let's go back to the trail. You saw the native – '

'We've been over that before,' said Falkner bitterly.

'We'll try it once again,' Warren told him. 'You say the native passed quite close to you when he went by. You mean that he stepped out of the path and circled past you . . .'

'No,' said Falkner, 'I don't mean that at all. I was the one who stepped out of the path.'

You must maintain human dignity, the manual said. Above all else, human dignity and human prestige must be upheld.

Kindness, yes. And helpfulness. And even brotherhood. But dignity was ahead of all.

And too often human dignity was human arrogance.

Human dignity did not allow you to step out of the path. It made the other thing step out and go around you. By inference, human dignity automatically assigned all other life to an inferior position.

'Mr Barnes,' said Warren, 'it was the laying on of hands.'

The man on the cot rolled his head on the pillow and looked at Warren, almost as if he were surprised to find him there. The thin lips worked in the pallid face and the words were weak and very slow in coming.

'Yes, Warren, it was the laying on of hands. A power these creatures have. Some Christ-like power that no human has.'

'But that was a divine power.'

'No, Warren,' said the chaplain, 'not necessarily. It wouldn't have to be. It might be a very real, a very human power, that goes with mental or spiritual perfection.'

Warren hunched forward on his stool. 'I can't believe it,' he said. 'I simply can't. Not those owl-eyed things.'

He looked up and glanced at the chaplain. Barnes' face had flushed with sudden fever and his breath was fluttery and shallow. His eyes were closed and he looked like a man already dead.

There had been that report by the third expedition's psychologist. It had said dignity and an exact code of honour and a rather primitive protocol. And that, of course, would fit.

But Man, intent upon his own dignity and his own prestige, had never accorded anyone else any dignity. He had been willing to be kind if his kindness were appropriately appreciated. He stood ready to help if his help were allowed to stand as a testament to his superiority. And here on Landro he had scarcely bothered to be either kind or helpful, never dreaming for a moment that the little owl-eyed native was anything other than a stone age creature that was a pest and nuisance and not to be taken too seriously even when he turned out, at times, to be something of a menace.

Until one day a frightened kid had stepped out of a path and let a native by.

'Courtesy,' said Warren. 'That's the answer: courtesy and the laying on of hands.'

He got up from the stool and walked out of the tent and met Falkner coming in.

'How is he?' Falkner asked.

Warren shook his head. 'Just like the others. It was late in coming, but it's just as bad.'

'Two of us,' said Falkner. 'Two of us left out of twenty-six.'

'Not two,' Warren told him. 'Just one. Just you.'

'But, sir, you're all . . .'

Warren shook his head.

'I have a headache,' he said. 'I'm beginning to sweat a little. My legs are wobbly.'

'Maybe . . .'

'I've seen it too many times,' said Warren, 'to kid myself about it.'

He reached out a hand, grasped the canvas and steadied himself.

'I didn't have a chance,' he said. 'I stepped out of no paths.'

GLEANERS

I

He went sneaking past the door.

The lettering on the door said: *Executive Vice President, Projects.*

And down in the lower left corner, *Hallock Spencer*, in very modest type.

That was him. He was Hallock Spencer.

But he wasn't going in that door. He had trouble enough already without going in. There'd be people waiting there for him. No one in particular – but people. And each of them with problems.

He ducked around the corner and went a step or two down the corridor until he came to another door that said *Private* on it.

It was unlocked. He went in.

A dowdy scarecrow in a faded, dusty toga sat tipped back in a chair, with his sandalled feet resting on Hallock Spencer's desk top. He wore a mouse-grey woollen cap upon his hairless skull and his ears stuck out like wings. A short sword, hanging from the belt that snugged in the toga, stood canted with its point resting on the carpet. There was dirt beneath his rather longish toenails and he hadn't shaved for days. He was a total slob.

'Hello, EJ,' said Spencer.

The man in the toga didn't take his feet off the desk. He didn't move at all. He just sat there.

'Sneaking in again,' he said.

Spencer put down his briefcase and hung up his hat.

'The reception room's a trap,' he said.

He sat down in the chair behind the desk and picked up the project schedule and had a look at it.

'What's the trouble, EJ?' he asked. 'You back already?'

'Haven't started yet. Not for another couple hours.'

'It says here,' said Spencer, flicking the schedule with a finger, 'that you're a Roman trader.'

'That's what I am,' said EJ. 'At least, Costumes says so. I hope to God they're right.'

'But the sword . . .'

'Pardner,' said EJ, 'back in Roman Britain, out on a Roman road, with a pack train loaded down with goods, a man has got to carry steel.'

He reached down and hoisted the sword into his lap. He regarded it with disfavour. 'But I don't mind telling you it's no great shakes of a weapon.'

'I suppose you'd feel safer with a tommy gun.'

EJ nodded glumly. 'Yes, I would.'

'Lacking that,' said Spencer, 'we do the best we can. You'll pack the finest steel in the second century. If that is any comfort.'

EJ just sat there with the sword across his lap. He was making up his mind to say something – it was written on his face. He was a silly-looking soul, with all those wiry whiskers and his ears way out to either side of him and the long black hairs that grew out of the lobes.

'Hal,' said EJ, finally making up his mind, 'I want out of this.'

Spencer stiffened in his chair. 'You can't do that!' he yelled. 'Time is your very life. You've been in it for a lot of years!'

'I don't mean out of Time. I mean out of Family Tree. I am sick of it.'

'You don't know what you're saying,' Spencer protested. 'Family Tree's not tough. You've been on a lot of worse ones. Family Tree's a snap. All you have to do is go back and talk to people or maybe check some records. You don't have to snitch a thing.'

'It's not the work,' said EJ. 'Sure, the work is easy. I don't mind the work. It's after I get back.'

'You mean the Wrightson-Graves.'

'That is what I mean. After every trip, she has me up to that fancy place of hers and I have to tell her all about her venerable ancestors . . .'

Spencer said, 'It's a valuable account. We have to service it.'

'I can't stand much more of it,' EJ insisted, stubbornly.

Spencer nodded. He knew just what EJ meant. He felt much the same.

Alma Wrightson-Graves was a formidable old dowager with a pouter-pigeon build and the erroneous conviction that she still retained much of her girlish charm. She was loaded down with cash, and also with jewels that were too costly and gaudy to be good taste. For years she'd shrieked down and bought off everyone around her until she firmly believed there was nothing in the world she couldn't have – if she was willing to pay enough for it.

And she was paying plenty for this family tree of hers. Spencer had often asked himself just why she wanted it. Back to the Conquest, sure – that made at least some sense. But not back to the caves. Not that Past, Inc., couldn't trace it that far for her if her cash continued to hold out. He thought, with a perverted satisfaction, that she couldn't have been happy with the last report or two, for the family had sunk back to abject peasantry.

He said as much to EJ. 'What does she want?' he asked. 'What does she expect?'

'I have a hunch,' EJ told him, 'that she has some hopes we'll find a connection back in Rome. God help us if we do. Then it could go on forever.'

Spencer grunted.

'Don't be too sure,' warned EJ. 'Roman officers being what they were I wouldn't bet against it.'

'If that should happen,' Spencer told him, 'I'll take you off the project. Assign someone else to carry out the Roman research. I'll tell the Wrightson-Graves you're not so hot on Rome – have a mental block or a psychic allergy or something that rejects indoctrination.'

'Thanks a lot,' said EJ, without much enthusiasm.

One by one, he took his dirty feet off the shiny desk and rose out of the chair.

'EJ?'

'Yes, Hal.'

'Just wondering. Have you ever hit a place where you felt that you should stay? Have you ever wondered if maybe you should stay?'

'Yeah, I guess so. Once or twice, perhaps. But I never did. You're thinking about Garson.'

'Garson for one. And all the others.'

'Maybe something happened to him. You get into tight spots. It's a simple matter to make a big mistake. Or the operator might have missed.'

'Our operators never miss,' snapped Spencer.

'Garson was a good man,' said EJ. a little sadly.

'Garson! It's not only Garson. It's all the . . .' Spencer stopped abruptly, for he'd run into it again. After all these years, he still kept running into it. No matter how he tried, it was something to which he could not reconcile himself – the disparity in time.

He saw that EJ was staring at him, with just the slightest crinkle that was not quite a smile at the corner of his mouth.

'You can't let it eat you,' said EJ 'You're not responsible. We take our chances. If it wasn't worth our while . . .'

'Oh, shut up!' said Spencer.

'Sure,' said EJ, 'you lose one of us every now and then. But it's no worse than any other business.'

'Not one every now and then,' said Spencer. 'There have been three of them in the last ten days.'

'Well, now,' said EJ, 'I lose track of them. There was Garson just the other day. And Taylor – how long ago was that?'

'Four days ago,' said Spencer.

'Four days,' said EJ, astonished. 'Is that all it was?'

Spencer snapped, 'For you it was three months or more. And do you remember Price? For you that was a year ago, but just ten days for me.'

EJ put up a dirty paw and scrubbed at the bristle on his chin. 'How time does fly!'

'Look,' said Spencer, miserably, 'this whole set-up is bad enough. Please don't make jokes about it.'

'Garside been giving you a hard time, maybe? Losing too many of the men?'

'Hell, no,' said Spencer, bitterly. 'You can always get more men. It's the machines that bother him. He keeps reminding me they cost a quarter million.'

EJ made a rude sound with his lips.

'Get out of here!' yelled Spencer. 'And see that you come home!'

EJ grinned and left. He gave the toga a girlish flirt as he went out the door.

II

Spencer told himself EJ was wrong. For whatever anyone might say, he, Hallock Spencer, was responsible. He ran the stinking show. He made up the schedules. He assigned the travellers and he sent them out. When there were mistakes or hitches, he was the one who answered. To himself, if no one else.

He got up and paced the floor, hands locked behind his back. Three men in the last ten days. And what had happened to them?

Possibly there was something to what Garside said, as well – Christopher Anson Garside, chief co-ordinator and a nasty man to handle, with his clipped, grey moustache and his clipped, grey voice and his clipped, grey business thinking.

For it was not men alone who did not come back. It was likewise the training and experience you had invested in those men. They lasted, Spencer told himself, a short time at the best without managing to get themselves killed off somewhere in the past, or deciding to squat down and settle in some other era they liked better than the present.

And the machines were something that could not be dismissed. Every time a man failed to return it meant another carrier lost. And the carriers *did* cost a quarter million – which wasn't something you could utterly forget.

Spencer went back to his desk and had another look at the schedule for the day. There was EJ bound for Roman Britain on the Family Tree project; Nickerson going back to the early Italian Renaissance to check up once again on the missing treasure in the Vatican; Hennessy off on his search once more for the lost documents in fifteenth-century Spain; Williams going out, he hoped, finally to snatch the mislaid Picasso, and a half dozen more. Not a massive schedule. But enough to spell out a fairly busy day.

He checked the men not on the projects list. A couple of them were on vacation. One was in Rehabilitation. Indoctrination had the rest of them.

He sat there, then, for the thousandth time, wondering what it would be like, really, to travel into time.

He'd heard hints of it from some of the travellers, but no more than hints, for they did not talk about it. Perhaps they did among themselves, when there were no outsiders present. Perhaps not even then. As if it were something that no man could quite describe. As if it were an experience that no man should discuss.

A haunting sense of unreality, the feeling that one was out of place, a hint of not quite belonging, of somehow standing, tip-toe, on the far edge of eternity.

It wore off after a time, of course, but apparently one was never entirely free of it. For the past, in some mysterious working of a principle yet unknown, was a world of wild enchantment.

Well, he had had his chance and flunked it.

But some day, he told himself, he could go into time. Not as a regular traveller, but as a vacationist – if he could snatch the necessary time to get ready for the trip. The trip, itself, of course, was no consideration so far as time might be concerned. It was Indoctrination and the briefing that was time-consuming.

He picked up the schedule again for another look. All of those who were going back this day were good men. There was no need to worry about any one of them.

He laid the schedule to one side and buzzed Miss Crane.

Miss Crane was a letter-perfect secretary, though she wasn't much to look at. She was a leathery old maid. She had her own way of doing things, and she could act very disapproving.

No choice of his, Spencer had inherited her fifteen years before. She had been with Past, Inc., before there was even a projects office. And, despite her lack of looks, her snippy attitude and her generally pessimistic view of life, she was indispensable.

She knew the projects job as well as he did. At times she let him know it. But she never forgot, never mislaid, never erred;

she ran an efficient office, always got her work done and it always was on time.

Spencer, dreaming at times of a lusher young replacement, knew that he was no more than dreaming. He couldn't do his job without Miss Crane in the outer office.

'You sneaked in again,' she accused him as soon as she'd closed the door.

'I suppose there's someone waiting.'

'There's a Dr Aldous Ravenholt,' she said. 'He's from Foundation for Humanity.'

Spencer flinched. There was no one worse to start a morning with than some pompous functionary from Humanity. They almost always figured that you owed them something. They thought the whole world owed them something.

'And there's a Mr Stewart Cabell. He's an applicant sent up by Personnel. Mr Spencer, don't you think . . .'

'No, I don't,' Spencer snapped at her. 'I know Personnel is sore. But I've been taking everyone they've been shovelling up here and see what happens. Three men gone in the last ten days. From now on, I'm taking a close look at everyone myself.'

She sniffed. It was a very nasty sniff.

'That's all?' asked Spencer, figuring that he couldn't be that lucky – just two of them.

'Also there's a Mr Boone Hudson. He's an elderly man who looks rather ill and he seems impatient. Perhaps you should see him first.'

Spencer might have, but not after she said that.

'I'll see Ravenholt,' he said. 'Any idea what he wants?'

'No, sir.'

'Well, send him in,' said Spencer. 'He'll probably want to chisel a slice of Time off me.'

Chisellers, he thought. I didn't know there were so many chisellers!

Aldous Ravenholt was a pompous man, well satisfied and smug. You could have buttered bread with the crease in his trousers. His handshake was professional and he had an automatic smile. He sat down in the chair that Spencer offered him with a self-assurance that was highly irritating.

'I came to talk with you,' he said precisely, 'about the pending proposal to investigate religious origins.'

Spencer winced mentally. It was a tender subject.

117

'Dr Ravenholt,' he said, 'that is a matter I have given a great deal of attention. Not myself alone, but my entire department.'

'That is what I've heard,' Ravenholt said drily. 'That is why I'm here. I understand you have tentatively decided not to go ahead with it.'

'Not tentatively,' said Spencer. 'Our decision has been made. I'm curious how you heard it.'

Ravenholt waved an airy hand, implying there was very little he did not know about. 'I presume the matter still is open to discussion.'

Spencer shook his head.

Ravenholt said, icily, 'I fail to see how you could summarily cut off an investigation so valid and so vital to all humanity.'

'Not summarily, Dr Ravenholt. We spent a lot of time on it. We made opinion samplings. We had an extensive check by Psych. We considered all the factors.'

'And your findings, Mr Spencer?'

'First of all,' said Spencer, just a little nettled, 'it would be too time-consuming. As you know, our licence specifies that we donate ten per cent of our operating time to public interest projects. This we are most meticulous in doing, although I don't mind telling you there's nothing that gives us greater headaches.'

'But that ten per cent . . .'

'If we took up this project you are urging, doctor, we'd use up all our public interest time for several years at least. That would mean no other programmes at all.'

'But surely you'll concede that no other proposal could be in a greater public interest.'

'That's not our findings,' Spencer told him. 'We took opinion samplings in every area on Earth, in all possible cross-sections. We came up with — sacrilege.'

'You're joking, Mr Spencer!'

'Not at all,' said Spencer. 'Our opinion-taking showed quite conclusively that any attempt to investigate world-wide religious origins would be viewed by the general public in a sacrilegious light. You and I, perhaps, could look upon it as research. We could resolve all our questioning by saying we sought no more nor less than truth. But the people of the world — the simple, common people of every sect and faith in the entire world — do not want the truth. They are satisfied with things just as they are. They're afraid we would upset a lot of the old, comfortable traditions. They call it sacrilege and it's partly that, of course, but it's likewise an instinctive defence reaction against upsetting their thinking. They have a faith to cling to. It has served them through the years and they don't want anyone to fool around with it.'

'I simply can't believe it,' said Ravenholt, aghast at such blind provincialism.

'I have the figures. I can show you.'

Dr Ravenholt waved his hand condescendingly and gracefully.

'If you say you have them, I am sure you have.'

He wasn't taking any chances of being proven wrong.

'Another thing,' said Spencer, 'is objectivity. How do you select the men to send back to observe the facts?'

'I am sure that we could get them. There are many men of the cloth, of every creed and faith, who would be amply qualified . . .'

'Those are just the ones we would never think of sending,' said Spencer. 'We need objectivity. Ideally, the kind of man we need is one who has no interest in religion, who has no formal training in it, one who is neither for it nor against it – and yet, we couldn't use that sort of man even if we found him. For to understand what is going on, he'd have to have a rather thorough briefing on what he was to look for. Once you trained him, he'd be bound to lose his objectivity. There is something about religion that forces one to take positions on it.'

'Now,' said Ravenholt, 'you are talking about the ideal investigative situation, not our own.'

'Well, all right, then,' conceded Spencer. 'Let's say we decide to do a slightly sloppy job. Who do we send then? Could any Christian, I ask you, no matter how poor a Christian he might be, safely be sent back to the days that Jesus spent on Earth? How could one be sure that even mediocre Christians would do no more than observe the facts? I tell you, Dr Ravenholt, we could not take the chance. What would happen, do you think, if we suddenly should have thirteen instead of twelve disciples? What if someone should try to rescue Jesus from the Cross? Worse yet, what if He actually were rescued? Where would Christianity be then? Would there be Christianity? Without the Crucifixion, would it ever have survived?'

'Your problem has a simple answer,' Ravenholt said coldly. 'Do not send a Christian.'

'Now we are really getting somewhere,' said Spencer. 'Let's send a Moslem to get the Christian facts and a Christian to track down the life of Buddha – and a Buddhist to investigate black magic in the Belgian Congo.'

'It could work,' said Ravenholt.

'It might work, but you wouldn't get objectivity. You'd get bias and, worse yet, perfectly honest misunderstanding.'

Ravenholt drummed impatient fingers on his well-creased knee. 'I can see your point,' he agreed, somewhat irritably, 'but there is something you have overlooked. The findings need not be released in their entirety to the public.'

'But if it's in the public interest? That's what our licence says.'

'Would it help,' asked Ravenholt, 'if I should offer certain funds which could be used to help defray the costs?'

'In such a case,' said Spencer, blandly, 'the requirement would not be met. It's either in the public interest, without any charge at all, or it's a commercial contract paid for at regular rates.'

'The obvious fact,' Ravenholt said flatly, 'is that you do not want to do this job. You may as well admit it.'

'Most cheerfully,' said Spencer. 'I willingly wouldn't touch it with a ten-foot pole. What worries me right now is why you're here.'

Ravenholt said, 'I thought that with the project about to be rejected, I possibly could serve as a sort of mediator.'

'You mean you thought we could be bribed.'

'Not at all,' said Ravenholt wrathfully. 'I was only recognizing that the project was perhaps a cut beyond what your licence calls for.'

'It's all of that,' said Spencer.

'I cannot fully understand your objection to it,' Ravenholt persisted.

'Dr Ravenholt,' said Spencer gently, 'how would you like to be responsible for the destruction of a faith?'

'But,' stammered Ravenholt, 'there is no such possibility . . .'

'Are you certain?' Spencer asked him. 'How certain are you, Dr Ravenholt? Even the black magic of the Congo?'

'Well, I – well, since you put it that way . . .'

'You see what I mean?' asked Spencer.

'But even so,' argued Ravenholt, 'there could be certain facts suppressed . . .'

'Come now! How long do you think you could keep it bottled up? Anyway, when Past, Inc., does a job,' Spencer told him firmly, 'it goes gunning for the truth. And when we learn it, we report it. That is the one excuse we have for our continuing existence. We have a certain project here – a personal, full-rate contract – in which we have traced a family tree for almost two thousand years. We have been forced to tell our client some unpleasant things. But we told them.'

'That's part of what I'm trying to convey to you,' shouted Ravenholt, shaken finally out of his ruthless calm. 'You are willing to embark upon the tracing of a family tree, but you refuse this!'

'And you are confusing two utterly different operations! This investigation of religious origins is a public interest matter. Family Tree is a private account for which we're being paid.'

Ravenholt rose angrily. 'We'll discuss this some other time, when we both can keep our temper.'

Spencer said wearily, 'It won't do any good. My mind is made up.'

'Mr Spencer,' Ravenholt said, nastily, 'I'm not without recourse.'

'Perhaps you're not. You can go above my head. If that is what you're thinking, I'll tell you something else: You'll carry out this project over my dead body. I will not, Dr Ravenholt, betray the faith of any people in the world.'

'We'll see,' said Ravenholt, still nasty.

'Now,' said Spencer, 'you're thinking that you can have me fired. Probably you could. Undoubtedly you know the very strings to pull. But it's no solution.'

'I would think,' said Ravenholt, 'it would be the perfect one.'

'I'd still fight you as a private citizen. I'd take it to the floor of the United Nations if I had to.'

They both were on their feet now, facing one another across the width of desk.

'I'm sorry,' Spencer said, 'that it turned out this way. But I meant everything I said.'

'So did I,' said Ravenholt, stalking out the door.

III

Spencer sat down slowly in his chair.

A swell way to start a day, he told himself.

But the guy had burned him up.

Miss Crane came in the door with a sheaf of papers for his desk.

'Mr Spencer, shall I send in Mr Hudson? He's been waiting a long time.'

'Is Hudson the applicant?'

'No, that is Mr Cabell.'

'Cabell is the man I want to see. Bring me his file.' She sniffed contemptuously and left.

Damn her, Spencer told himself, I'll see who I want to see when I want to see them!

He was astounded at the violence of his thought. What was wrong with him? Nothing was going right. Couldn't he get along with anyone any more?

Too tensed up, he thought. Too many things to do, too much to worry over.

Maybe what he ought to do was walk out into Operations and step into a carrier for a long vacation. Back to the Old Stone Age, which would require no Indoctrination. There wouldn't be too many people, perhaps none at all. But there'd be mosquitoes. And cave bears. And sabre-tooths and perhaps a lot of other things equally obnoxious. And he'd have to get some camping stuff together and – oh, the hell with it!

But it was not a bad idea.

He'd thought about it often. Some day he would do it. Meanwhile, he picked up the sheaf of papers Miss Crane had dropped upon his desk.

They were the daily batch of future assignments dreamed up by the Dirty Tricks department. There was always trouble in them. He felt himself go tense as he picked them up.

The first one was a routine enough assignment – an investigation of some tributes paid the Goths by Rome. There was, it seemed, a legend that the treasure had been buried somewhere in the Alps. It might never have been recovered. That was S.O.P., checking up on buried treasure.

But the second paper . . .

'Miss Crane!' he yelled.

She was coming through the door, with a file clutched in her hand. Her face changed not a whit at his yelp of anguish; she was used to it.

'What is the matter, Mr Spencer?' she inquired, at least three degrees too calmly.

Spencer banged his fist down on the pile of sheets. 'They can't do this to me! I won't stand for it. Get Rogers on the phone!'

'Yes, sir.'

'No, wait a minute there,' Spencer interrupted grimly. 'This I can do better personal. I'll go up and see him. In fact, I'll take him apart barehanded.'

'But there are those people waiting . . .'

'Let them wait for a while. It will make them humble.'

He snatched up the assignment sheet and went striding out the door. He shunned the elevator. He climbed two flights of stairs. He went in a door marked *Evaluation*.

Rogers was sitting tilted back, with his feet up on the desk top, staring at the ceiling.

He glanced at Spencer with a bland concern. He took his feet down off the desk and sat forward in his chair.

'Well? What's the matter this time?'

'This!' said Spencer, throwing the sheet down in front of him.

Rogers poked it with a delicate finger. 'Nothing difficult there. Just a little ingenuity . . .'

'Nothing difficult!' howled Spencer. 'Movies of Nero's fire in Rome!'

Rogers sighed. 'This movie outfit will pay us plenty for it.'

'And there's nothing to it. One of my men can just walk out into the burning streets of Rome and set up a movie camera in an age where the principle of the camera hasn't yet been thought of.'

'Well, I said it would call for some ingenuity,' said Rogers. 'Look, there'll be a lot of people running, carrying stuff, trying to save themselves and anything they can. They won't pay any attention to your man. He can cover the camera with something so that it will look . . .'

'It'll be an ugly crowd,' insisted Spencer. 'It won't like the city being burned. There'll be rumours that the Christians are the ones who set the fire. That crowd will be looking for suspicious characters.'

'There's always an element of danger,' Rogers pointed out.

'Not as dangerous as this!' said Spencer, testily. 'Not deliberately asking for it. And there is something else.'

'Like what?'

'Like introducing an advanced technology to the past. If that crowd beat up my man and busted the camera . . .'

Rogers shrugged. 'What difference if they did? They could make nothing of it.'

'Maybe. But what I'm really worried about,' Spencer persisted, 'is what the watchdog group would say when they audit our records. It would have to be worth an awful lot of money before I'd take a chance.'

'Believe me, it is worth a lot of money. And it would open up a new field for us. That's why I liked it.'

'You guys in Dirty Tricks,' said Spencer, bitterly, 'just don't give a damn. You'll hand us anything . . .'

'Not everything,' said Rogers. 'Sales pushed us pretty hard on this one . . .'

'Sales!' spat Spencer, contempt in his voice.

'There was a woman in here the other day,' said Rogers. 'She wanted to send her two children to their great-great-great-grandfather's farm back in the nineteenth century. For a vacation, mind you. A summer in the country in another century. Said it would be educational and quite relaxing for them. Said the old folks would understand and be glad to have them once we had explained.'

Rogers sighed. 'I had quite a session with her. She pooh-poohed our regulations. She said . . .'

'You passed up a good one there,' Spencer said sarcastically. 'That would have opened up another field – vacations in the past. I can see it now. Family reunions with old friends and neighbours foregathering across the centuries.'

'You think you are the only one who has his troubles.'

124

'I am bleeding for you,' Spencer told him.

'There's a TV outfit,' Rogers said, 'that wants interviews with Napoleon and Caesar and Alexander and all the rest of those ancient bigshots. There are hunters who want to go back into the primordial wilderness to get a spot of shooting. There are universities that want to send teams of investigators back . . .'

'You know that all of that is out,' said Spencer. 'The only ones we can send back are travellers we have trained.'

'There've been times.'

'Oh, sure, a few. But only when we got a special dispensation. And we sent along so many travellers to guard them that it was an expedition instead of a simple little study group.'

Spencer got up from his chair. 'Well, what about this latest brainstorm?'

Rogers picked up the offending assignment sheet and tossed it into an overflowing basket.

'I'll go down to Sales, with tears streaming down my cheeks . . .'

'Thanks,' said Spencer and went out.

IV

Back in his office, he sat down at the desk and picked up the file on Cabell.

The squawk box gibbered at him. He thumbed up the lever.

'What is it?'

'Operations, Hal. Williams just got back. Everything's okay; he snagged the Picasso without any trouble. Only took six weeks.'

'Six weeks!' Spencer yelled. 'He could have painted it himself in that time!'

'There were complications.'

'Is there any time there aren't?'

'It's a good one, Hal. Not damaged. Worth a hunk of dough.'

'Okay,' said Spencer, 'take it down to Customs and let them run it through. The good old government must be paid its duty. And what about the others?'

'Nickerson will be leaving in just a little while.'

'And EJ?'

'He's fussy about the time fix. He is telling Doug . . .'

'Look,' yelled Spencer wrathfully, 'you tell him for me that the fix is Doug's job. Doug knows more about it than EJ ever will. When Doug says it's time to hop, EJ hops, funny cap and all.'

He snapped down the lever and turned back to the Cabell file, sitting quietly for a moment to let his blood pressure simmer down.

He got worked up too easily, he told himself. He blew his top too much. But there never was a job with so many aggravations!

He opened the folder and ran through the Cabell file.

Stewart Belmont Cabell, 27, unmarried, excellent references, a doctorate in sociology from an ivy college. A uniformly high score in all the tests, including attitude, and an astonishing IQ. Unqualifiedly recommended for employment as a traveller.

Spencer closed the file and pushed it to one side.

'Send Mr Cabell in,' he told Miss Crane.

Cabell was a lanky man, awkward in his movements; he seemed younger than he was. There was a certain shyness in his manner when Spencer shook his hand and pointed out a chair.

Cabell sat and tried, without success, to make himself at ease.

'So you want to come in with us,' said Spencer. 'I suppose you know what you are doing.'

'Yes, sir,' said young Cabell. 'I know all about it. Or perhaps I'd better say . . .'

He stammered and stopped talking.

'It's all right,' said Spencer. 'I take it you want this very much.'

Cabell nodded.

'I know how it is. You almost have the feeling you'll die if you can't do it.'

And he remembered, sitting there, how it had been with him – the terrible, tearing heartache when he'd been rejected as a traveller, and how he had stuck on regardless of that hurt and disappointment. First as operator; then as operations superintendent; finally to this desk, with all its many headaches.

'Not,' he said, 'that I have ever travelled.'

'I didn't know that, sir.'

'I wasn't good enough. My attitudes were wrong.'

126

And he saw the old hope and hunger in the eyes of the man across the desk – and something else besides. Something vaguely disturbing.

'It's not all fun,' he said, a shade more harshly than he had meant to make it. 'At first there's the romance and the glitter, but that soon wears off. It becomes a job. Sometimes a bitter one.'

He paused and looked at Cabell and the queer, disturbing light still was shining in his eyes.

'You should know,' he said, deliberately harsh this time, 'that if you come in with us you'll probably be dead of advanced old age in five years.'

Cabell nodded unconcernedly. 'I know that, sir. The people down in Personnel explained it all to me.'

'Good,' said Spencer. 'I suspect at times that Personnel makes a rather shabby explanation. They tell you just enough to make it sound convincing, but they do not tell it all. They are far too anxious to keep us well supplied. We're always short of travellers; we run through them too fast.'

He paused and looked at the man again. There was no change in him.

'We have certain regulations,' Spencer told him. 'They aren't made so much by Past, Inc., as by the job itself. You cannot have any settled sort of life. You live out your life in pieces, like a patchwork quilt, hopping from neighbourhood to neighbourhood, and those neighbourhoods all many years apart. There is no actual rule against it, but none of our travellers has ever married. It would be impossible. In five years the man would die of old age and his wife would still be young.'

'I think I understand, sir.'

'Actually,' Spencer said, 'it's a very simple matter of simple economics. We cannot afford to have either our machines or men tied up for any length of time. So while a man may be gone a week, a month, or years, the machine comes back, with him inside of it, sixty seconds after he has left. That sixty seconds is an arbitrary period; it could be a single second, it could be an hour or day or anything we wanted. One minute has seemed a practical period.'

'And,' asked Cabell, 'if it does not come back within that minute?'

'Then it never will.'

'It sometimes happens?'

'Of course it happens. Time travelling is no picnic. Every time a man goes back he is betting his life that he can get along in an environment which is as totally alien, in some instances, as another planet. We help him in every way we can, of course. We make it our business to see that he is well briefed and Indoctrinated and as well equipped as it is possible to make him. He is taught the languages he is likely to require. He is clothed properly. But there are instances when we simply do not know the little vital details which mean survival. Sometimes we learn them later when our man comes back and tells us. Usually he is quite profane about it. And some we don't find out about at all. The man does not come back.'

'One would think,' said Cabell, 'that you would like to scare me out.'

'No! I tell you this because I want no misunderstanding. It costs a lot to train a traveller. We must get our costs back. We do not want a man who will stay with us just a little while. We don't want a year or two from you; we want your entire life. We'll take you and we'll wring you dry of every minute . . .'

'I can assure you, sir . . .'

'We send you where we want you,' Spencer said, 'and although we have no control of you once you've left, we expect that you'll not fool around. Not that you won't came back inside of sixty seconds – naturally you will, if you come back at all. But we want you to come back as young as possible. Past, Inc., is a pure commercial venture. We'll squeeze all the trips we possibly can out of you.'

'I understand all this,' said Cabell, 'but Personnel explained it would be to my advantage, too.'

'That is true, of course, but it'll not take you long to find that money is of slight moment to a traveller. Since you have no family, or we would hope you haven't, what would you need it for? The only leisure time you'll have is a six weeks' annual leave and you can earn enough in a trip or two to spend that leave in utmost luxury or the deepest vice.

'Most of the men, however, don't even bother to do that. They just wander off and get re-acquainted with the era they were born into. Vice and luxury in this present century has but slight appeal to them after all the hell they've raised in past centuries at the company's expense.'

'You are kidding, sir.'

'Well, maybe just a little. But in certain cases that I have in mind, it is the honest truth.'

Spencer stared across at Cabell.

'None of this bothers you?' he asked.

'Not a thing so far.'

'There's just one thing else, Mr Cabell, that you should know about. That is the need – the imperative, crying need for objectivity. When you go into the past, you take no part in it. You do not interfere. *You must not get involved.*'

'That should not be hard.'

'I warn you, Mr Cabell, that it requires moral stamina. The man who travels in time has terrible power. And there's something about the feel of power that makes it almost compulsive for a man to use it. Hand in hand with that power is the temptation to take a hand in history. To wield a judicious knife, to say a word that needs saying very badly. To save a life that, given a few more years of time, might have pushed the human race an extra step toward greatness.'

'It might be hard,' admitted Cabell.

Spencer nodded. 'So far as I know, Mr Cabell, no one has ever succumbed to these temptations. But I live in terror of the day when someone does.'

And he wondered as he said it how much he might be talking through his hat, might be whistling past the graveyard. For surely there must by now have been some interference.

What about the men who had not come back?

Some of them undoubtedly had died. But surely some had stayed. And wasn't staying back there the worst form of intervention? What were the implications, he wondered, of a child born out of time – a child that had not been born before, that should never have been born? The children of that child and the children of those children – they would be a thread of temporal interference reaching through the ages.

Cabell asked: 'Is there something wrong, sir?'

'No. I was just thinking that the time will surely come, some day, when we work out a formula for safely interfering in the past. And when that happens, our responsibilities will be even greater than the ones that we face now. For then we'll have licence for intervening, but will in turn be placed under certain strictures to use that power of intervention only for the best. I can't imagine what sort of principle it will be, you understand. But I am sure that soon or late we will arrive at it.

'And perhaps, too, we'll work out another formula which will allow us to venture to the future.'

He shook his head and thought: How like an old man, to shake your head in resigned puzzlement. But he was not an old man – not very old, at least.

'At the moment,' he said, 'we are little more than gleaners. We go into the past to pick up the gleanings – the things they lost or threw away. We have made up certain rules to make sure that we never touch the sheaves, but only the ear of wheat left lying on the ground.'

'Like the Alexandria manuscripts?'

'Well, yes, I would suppose so – although grabbing all those manuscripts and books was inspired entirely by a sordid profit motive. We could just as easily have copied them. Some of them we did; but the originals themselves represented a tremendous sum of money. I would hate to tell you what Harvard paid us for those manuscripts. Although, when you think of it,' Spencer said, reflectively. 'I'm not sure they weren't worth every cent of it. It called for the closest planning and split-second co-ordinating and we used every man we had. For, you see, we couldn't grab the stuff until it was on the verge of burning. We couldn't deprive even so much as a single person the chance of even glancing at a single manuscript. We can't lift a thing until it's lost. That's an iron-bound rule.

'Now, you take the Ely tapestry. We waited for years, going back and checking, until we were quite sure that it was finally lost. We knew it was going to be lost, you understand. But we

couldn't touch it until it was lost for good. Then we heisted it.'
He waved a hand. 'I talk too much. I am boring you.'

'Mr Spencer, sir,' protested Cabell, 'talk like yours could never bore me. This is something I have dreamed of. I can't tell you how happy . . .'

Spencer raised a hand to stop him. 'Not so fast. You aren't hired yet.'

'But Mr Jensen down in Personnel . . .'

'I know what Jensen said. But the final word is mine.'

'What have I done wrong?' asked Cabell.

'You have done nothing wrong. Come back this afternoon.'

'But, Mr Spencer, if only you could tell me . . .'

'I want to think about you. See me after lunch.'

Cabell unfolded upward from his chair and he was ill at ease. 'That man who was in ahead of me . . .'

'Yes. What about him?'

'He seemed quite angry, sir. As if he might be thinking of making trouble for you.'

Spencer said angrily, 'And that's none of your damn business!'

Cabell stood his ground. 'I was only going to say, sir, that I recognized him.'

'So?'

'If he did try to cause you trouble, sir, it might be worth your while to investigate his association with a stripper down at the Golden Hour. Her name is Silver Starr.'

Spencer stared at Cabell without saying anything.

The man edged toward the door.

He put out his hand to grasp the knob, then turned back to Spencer. 'Perhaps that's not actually her name, but it's fine for advertising – Silver Starr at the Golden Hour. The Golden Hour is located at . . .'

'Mr Cabell,' Spencer said, 'I've been at the Golden Hour.'

The impudent punk! What did he figure he was doing – buying his way in?

He sat quietly for a moment after Cabell had gone out, cooling down a bit, wondering about the man. There had been something about him that had been disturbing. That look in his eyes, for one thing. And the awkwardness and shyness didn't ring quite true. As if it had been an act of some sort. But why, in the name of God, should anyone put on such an act when it would be quite clearly to his disadvantage?

You're psycho, Spencer told himself. You're getting so you jump at every shadow, sight a lurking figure behind every bush.

Two down, he thought, and another one to see – that is, if more had not piled into the office and were out there waiting for him.

He reached out his hand to press the buzzer. But before his finger touched it, the back door of the office suddenly burst open. A wild-eyed man came stumbling through it. He had something white and wriggly clutched within his arms. He dumped the white and wriggly thing on Hallock Spencer's desk and unhappily stepped back.

It was a rabbit – a white rabbit with a great pink ribbon tied around its neck in a fancy bow.

Spencer glanced up, startled, at the man who'd brought the rabbit.

'Ackermann,' he shouted. 'For Chrissake, Ackermann, what is the matter with you? It isn't Easter yet!'

Ackermann worked his mouth in a painful manner and his Adam's apple went bobbing up and down. But he made no words come out.

'Come on, man! What is it?'

Ackermann got his voice back. 'It's Nickerson!' he blurted.

'OK, so Nickerson brought a rabbit back . . .'

'He didn't bring it back, sir. It came all by itself!'

'And Nickerson?'

Ackermann shook his head. 'There was just the rabbit.'

Spencer had started to get up from the chair. Now he sat back down again, harder than intended.

'There's an envelope, sir, tied to the rabbit's bow.'

'So I see,' said Spencer, absently. But he felt the coldness running through him.

The rabbit hoisted itself around until it was face to face with Spencer. It flapped an ear, wiggled its pink nose at him, put its head carefully to one side and lifted a deliberate hind leg to scratch a flea.

He pivoted in his chair and watched the operator sidle

through the door. Three men lost in the last ten days. And now there was a fourth.

But this time, at least, he'd got back the carrier. The rabbit had brought back the carrier. Any living thing, once the mechanism had been rigged, by its very presence would have brought back the carrier. It need not be a man.

But Nickerson! Nickerson was one of the best there were. If a man could not depend on Nickerson, there was no one that he could.

He turned back to the desk and reached for the rabbit. It didn't try to get away. He slipped out the folded sheet of paper and broke the blob of sealing wax. The paper was so stiff and heavy that it crackled as he smoothed it.

The ink was dead black and the script cramped. No fountain pen, thought Spencer – nothing but a goose quill.

The letter was addressed to him. It said:

> Dear Hal: I have no logical excuse and I'll attempt no explanation. I have found a sense of springtime and cannot compel myself to leave it. You have your carrier and that is better than any of the others ever did for you. The rabbit will not mind. A rabbit knows no time. Be kind to him – for he is no coarse, wild hare of the briery fields, but a loving pet. Nick.

Inadequate, thought Spencer, staring at the note, with its scrawly black more like a cabalistic pattern than a communication.

He had found a sense of springtime. What did he mean by that? A springtime of the heart? A springtime of the spirit? That might well be it, for Nickerson had gone to Italy in the early Renaissance. A springtime of the spirit and the sense of great beginnings. And perhaps that wasn't all of it. Would there be as well a certain sense of spiritual security in that smaller world – a world that tinkered with no time, that reached toward no stars?

The buzzer sounded softly.

Spencer tipped up the lever on the intercom. 'Yes, Miss Crane?'

'Mr Garside on the phone.'

The rabbit was nibbling at the phone cord. Spencer pushed him to one side. 'Yes, Chris.'

The grey, clipped voice said: 'Hal, what's with you and Ravenholt? He gave me a bad half hour.'

'It was Project God.'

'Yes, he told me that. He threatened to raise a howl about the ethics of our magazine project.'

'He can't do that,' protested Spencer. 'He'd have no grounds at all. That one is clean. It has the green light from Legal and from Ethics and the review board gave its blessing. It's simply historical reporting. Eyewitness from the battle of Gettysburg, fashion notes on the spot from the time of Queen Victoria – it's the biggest thing we've tackled. Its promotional value alone, aside from the money that we'll make . . .'

'Yes, I know,' said Garside, tiredly. 'All of that is true. But I don't want to get into a hassle with anyone – particularly not with Ravenholt. We have too many irons in the fire right now for anything unfavourable to pop. And Ravenholt can be a terribly dirty fighter.'

'Look, Chris. I can take care of Ravenholt.'

'I knew you would. What is more, you'd better.'

'And,' demanded Spencer, bristling, 'what do you mean by that?'

'Well, frankly, Hal, your record doesn't look too good. You've been having trouble . . .'

'You mean the men we've lost.'

'And the machines,' said Garside. 'You're all the time forgetting – a machine costs a quarter million.'

'And the men?' asked Spencer bitterly. 'Perhaps you think they're comparatively cheap.'

'I don't suppose,' said Garside blandly, 'that you can place an actual value on a human life.'

'We lost another one today,' said Spencer. 'I imagine you'll be happy to know that he was loyal beyond the call of duty. He sent a rabbit back and the machine is safe and sound.'

'Hal,' said Garside, sternly, 'this is something we can discuss at some later time. Right now I'm concerned with Ravenholt. If you'd go and apologize to him and try to fix things up . . .'

'Apologize!' exploded Spencer. 'I know a better way than

134

that. He's been shacking with a stripper down at the Golden Hour. By the time I get through . . .'

'Hal!' yelled Garside. 'You can't do a thing like that! You can't involve Past, Inc., in anything like that! Why, it isn't decent!'

'You mean it's dirty,' Spencer said. 'No dirtier than Ravenholt. Who is he fronting for?'

'It makes no difference. Young man . . .'

'Don't young man me,' yelled Spencer. 'I've got troubles enough without being patronized.'

'Perhaps your troubles are too much for you,' said Garside, speaking very grey and clipped. 'Perhaps we ought to find another man.'

'Do it then!' yelled Spencer. 'Don't just sit there shooting off your face. Come on down and fire me!'

He slammed the receiver down into its cradle and sat shivering with rage.

Damn Garside, he thought. To hell with Past, Inc. He'd taken all he could!

Still, it was a lousy way to end after fifteen years. It was a stinking thing to happen. Maybe he ought to have kept his mouth shut, kept his temper down, played it sweet and smooth.

Perhaps, he could have done it differently. He could have assured Garside he'd take care of Ravenholt without saying anything about Silver Starr. And why had he grabbed hold so trustfully of what Cabell had told him that moment before leaving? What could Cabell know about it? In just a little while now he'd have to check if there were anyone by the name of Silver Starr down at the Golden Hour.

Meanwhile there was work to do. Hudson now, he thought.

He reached for the buzzer.

But his finger never touched it. Once more the back door burst open with a smashing rattle and a man came tearing in. It was Douglas Marshall, operator for EJ's machine.

'Hal,' he gasped, 'you'd better come. EJ's really tore it!'

VI

Spencer didn't ask a question. One look at Doug's face was quite enough to tell him the news was very bad. He bounced out of his chair and rushed through the door, close on the operator's heels.

They tore down the corridor and turned left into Operations, with the rows of bulgy, bulky carriers lined against the wall.

Down at the far end a small crowd of operators and mechanics formed a ragged circle and from the centre of the circle came the sound of ribald song. The words were not intelligible.

Spencer strode forward angrily and pushed through the circle. There, in the centre of it, was EJ and another person – a filthy, bearded, boisterous barbarian wrapped in a mangy bearskin and with a tremendous sword strapped about his middle.

The barbarian had a smallish keg tilted to his mouth. The keg was gurgling; he was drinking from it, but he was missing some as well, for streams of pale, brown liquid were running down his front.

'EJ!' yelled Spencer.

At the shout, the barbarian jerked the keg down from his face and tucked it hurriedly underneath his arm. With a big and dirty hand, he mopped the whiskers adjacent to his mouth.

EJ stumbled forward and threw his arms around Spencer's neck, laughing all the while.

Spencer jerked EJ loose and pushed him, stumbling, backwards.

'EJ!' he yelled. 'What is so damn funny?'

EJ managed to stop stumbling backwards. He tried to pull himself together, but he couldn't because he still was laughing hard.

The barbarian stepped forward and thrust the keg into Spencer's hands, shouting something at him in a convivial tone of voice and pantomiming with his hands that the keg had stuff to drink.

EJ made an exaggerated thumb at the gent in bearskin. 'Hal, it wasn't any Roman officer!' Then he went off into gales of laughter once again.

The barbarian started to laugh, too, uproariously, throwing back his head and bellowing in great peals of laughter that shook the very room.

EJ staggered over and they fell into one another's arms, guffawing happily and pounding one another on the back. Somehow they got tangled up. They lost their balance. They fell down on the floor and sat there, the two of them, looking up at the men around them.

'Now!' Spencer roared at EJ.

EJ clapped the man in bearskin a resounding whack upon his hairy shoulder. 'Just bringing back the Wrightson-Graves her far-removed grand-pappy. I can't wait to see her face when I take him up there!'

'Oh, my God!' said Spencer. He turned around and thrust the dripping keg into someone's hands.

He snapped, 'Don't let them get away. Put them somewhere where they can sleep it off.'

A hand grabbed him by the arm and there was Douglas Marshall, sweating. 'We got to send him back, Chief,' said Doug. 'EJ's got to take him back.'

Spencer shook his head. 'I don't know if we can. I'll put it up to Legal. Just keep them here, and tell the boys. Tell them if one of them so much as whispers . . .'

'I'll do my best,' said Doug. 'But I don't know. They're a bunch of blabbermouths.'

Spencer jerked away and sprinted for the corridor.

What a day, he thought. What a loused-up day!

He charged down the corridor and saw that the door marked *Private* was closed. He skidded almost to a halt, reaching for the knob, when the door flew open. Miss Crane came tearing out.

She slammed into him head-on. Both of them bounced back, Miss Crane's spectacles knocked at a crazy angle by the impact.

'Mr Spencer,' she wailed. 'Mr Spencer, something awful's happened! Remember Mr Hudson?'

She stepped back out of his way. He sprang inside and slammed the door behind him. 'As if I ever could forget him,' he said bitterly.

Said Miss Crane, 'Mr Hudson's dead!'

Spencer stood stricken.

Miss Crane raged, 'If only you had seen him when *I* wanted you to! If you hadn't kept him waiting out there . . .'

'Now, look here . . .'

'He got up finally,' said Miss Crane, 'and his face was red. He was angry. I don't blame him, Mr Spencer.'

'You mean he died right here?'

'He said to me, "Tell your Mr Spencer . . ." and that's as far as he ever got. He sort of lurched and caught with his hand at the edge of the desk to support himself, but his hand slipped off and he folded up and . . .'

Spencer waited for no more. He went in three quick steps across the office and out into the reception room.

There was Mr Hudson, huddled on the carpet.

He looked startlingly like a limp rag-doll. One blue-veined hand was stretched out ahead of him. The portfolio that it had held lay just beyond the fingertips, as if even in his death Mr Hudson might be stretching out his hand to it. His jacket was hunched across the shoulders. The collar of his white shirt, Spencer saw, was ragged.

Spencer went slowly across the floor and knelt down beside the man. He put his ear down on the body.

There was no sound at all.

'Mr Spencer.' Miss Crane was standing in the doorway, still terrified but enjoying it a lot. Not in all her years of being secretary had anything like this happened. Not in all her life. It would keep her supplied with conversation for many, many years.

'Lock the door,' said Spencer, 'so no one can come strolling in. Then phone the police.'

'The police!'

'Miss Crane,' said Spencer, sharply.

She walked around him and the body on the floor, edging close against the wall.

'Call Legal, too,' said Spencer.

He stayed squatting on the floor, staring at the man who lay there and wondering how it had happened. Heart attack, most likely. Miss Crane had said that he looked ill – and had urged that he see him first, ahead of the other two.

And if one were looking for a man to blame for what had

138

happened here, Spencer told himself, they might have but little trouble fastening it on him.

If Hudson had not had to wait, growing angrier and more upset as the time slipped past, this might not have happened.

Hudson had waited in this room, a sick and impatient man, and finally an angry one – and what had he waited for?

Spencer studied the rag-doll of a man slumped upon the carpet, the thinning hair atop his head, the thick-lensed spectacles bent and twisted in the fall, the bony, blue-veined hands. He wondered what such a man might have expected from Past, Inc.

Spencer started to get up and lost his balance as he did, his left hand going out behind him to prop himself erect.

And beneath the spread-out palm there was something cool and smooth. Without looking, he knew what it was. Hudson's portfolio!

The answer might be there!

Miss Crane was at the door, locking it. There was no one else.

With a swift sweep of his hand, Spencer skidded the portfolio in the direction of the doorway that led into his office.

He got smoothly to his feet and turned. The portfolio lay halfway through the doorway. In one quick stride he reached it and nudged it with his foot, inside and out of sight.

He heard the snick of the lock falling home and Miss Crane turned around.

'The police first, or Legal, Mr Spencer?'

'The police, I'd think,' said Spencer.

He stepped within his office and swung the door so that it came within an inch of closing. Then he snatched the portfolio off the floor and hurried to his desk.

He put it on his desk and zipped it open and there were three sheaves of paper, each of the sheaves paper-clipped together.

The first bore the legend at the top of the first page: *A Study of Ethics Involved in Travelling in Time*. And after that page upon page of typescript, heavily underlined and edited with a neat red pencil.

And the second, a thin one, with no legend, and composed of sheets of unneatly scribbled notes.

And the third, once again typed, with carefully drawn

diagrams and charts, and the heading: *A New Concept of the Mechanics of Time Travel*.

Spencer sucked in his breath and bent above the paper, his eyes trying to gallop along the lines of type, but forced to go too fast to really catch the meaning.

For he had to get the portfolio back where it had been and he had to do it without being seen. It was not his to touch. The police might become difficult if they found he'd rifled it. And when he put it back, it must have something in it. A man would hardly come to see him with an empty portfolio.

In the outer office, he heard Miss Crane talking. He made a quick decision.

He swept the second and third sheaf of papers into the top drawer of his desk. Leaving the first sheaf on time-travel ethics in the portfolio, he zipped it shut again.

That would satisfy the cops. He held the portfolio in his left hand, letting his arm hang along his side, and stepped to the doorway, shielding the left side of his body and the portfolio.

Miss Crane was on the phone, her face turned away from him.

He dropped the portfolio on the carpeting, just beyond the outstretched fingers of the dead man.

Miss Crane put down the phone and saw him standing there.

'The police will be right over,' she said. 'Now I'll call Mr Hawkes in Legal.'

'Thanks,' said Spencer. 'I'll go through some papers while we're waiting.'

VII

Back at his desk, he took out the pile of papers that said: *A New Concept of the Mechanics of Time Travel*. The name on it was Boone Hudson.

He settled down to read, first with mounting wonderment, then with a strange, cold excitement – for here, at last, was the very thing that would at once erase the basic headache of Past, Inc.

No longer would one face the nightmare of good travellers wearing out in a few years' time.

No longer would a man go into time a young man and return

140

sixty seconds later with the beginning lines of age showing on his face. No longer would one watch one's friends age visibly from month to month.

For they would no longer be dealing in men, but in the patterns of those men.

Matter transference, Spencer told himself. You could probably call it that, anyway. A man would be sent into the past; but the carrier would not move physically into time as it moved now. It would project a pattern of itself and the man within it, materializing at the target point. And within the carrier – the basic carrier, the prime carrier, the parent carrier which would remain in present time – there'd be another pattern, a duplicate pattern of the man sent into time.

When the man returned to present time, he would not return as he was at that moment in the past, but as the pattern within the waiting carrier said he *had* been when he'd travelled into time.

He'd step out of the carrier exactly as he had stepped into it, not older by a second – actually a minute younger than he would have been! For he did not have to account for that sixty seconds between leaving and returning.

For years, Past, Inc.'s, own research department had been seeking for the answer to the problem, without even coming close. And now a stranger had come unheralded and sat hunched in the reception room, with the portfolio cradled on his knee, and he had the answer, but he'd been forced to wait.

He'd waited and he'd waited and finally he had died.

There was a tapping at the door of the outer office. He heard Miss Crane cross the room to open it.

Spencer pulled out a desk drawer and hurriedly shoved the papers into it. Then he stood up from the desk and walked around it to go into the outer office.

Ross Hawkes, head of Past, Inc.'s legal department, was standing just beyond the body on the carpet, staring down at it.

'Hello, Ross,' said Spencer. 'An unpleasant business here.'

Hawkes looked up at him, puzzled. His pale blue eyes glittered behind the neat and precise spectacles, his snow white hair matching the pallor of his face.

'But what was Dan'l doing here?' he asked.

141

'Dan'l?' Spencer demanded. 'His name happened to be Boone Hudson.'

'Yes, I know,' said Hawkes. 'But the boys all called him Dan'l – Dan'l Boone, you understand. Sometimes he didn't like it. He worked in Research. We had to fire him, fifteen, sixteen years ago. The only reason that I recognized him was that we had some trouble. He had an idea he would like to sue us.'

Spencer nodded. 'Thanks. I see,' he said.

He was halfway to his office door when he turned back.

'One thing, Ross. What did we fire him for?'

'I don't recall exactly. He disregarded his assignment, went off on some other tangent. Matter transference, I think.'

Spencer said, 'That's the way it goes.'

He went back into the office, locked his desk and went out the back way.

In the parking lot, he backed out his car and went slowly down the street. A police cruiser was parked in front of the building and two officers were getting out. An ambulance was pulling in behind the cruiser.

So, thought Spencer, they had fired Hudson fifteen years ago, because he had some sort of crazy idea about matter transference and wouldn't stick to business. And to this very day, Research was going quietly mad trying to solve a problem that Hudson could have put into their laps years ago, if they had kept him on.

Spencer tried to imagine how those fifteen years must have been for Hudson, more than likely working all the time on this quiet insanity of his. And how, finally, he had gotten it and had made sure of it and then had gone down to Past, Inc., to rub their noses in it.

Exactly as he, Hallock Spencer, now would rub their noses in it.

Greenwich Street was a quiet residential street of genteel poverty, with small and older houses. Despite the smallness of the houses and their age, and in some cases their unkemptness, there was a certain solid pride and respectability about them.

The address on the manuscript was 241 Greenwich. It was a squat brown house surrounded by a crumbling picket fence. The yard was full of flowers. Even so, it had the look of a house that had no one living in it.

142

Spencer edged through the sagging gate and up the walk, made small by the flowers that encroached upon it. He went up the rickety stairs to the shaky porch and, since there was no bell, rapped on the closed front door.

There was no answer. He tried the knob and it turned. He pushed the door part way open and edged into the silent hall.

'Hello,' he called. 'Anyone at home?'

He waited. There wasn't.

He walked from the hall into the living room and stood to look around him at the Spartan, almost monklike existence of the man who'd lived there.

It was evident that Hudson had lived alone, for the room bore all the signs of a lone man's camping. There was a cot against one wall, a dirty shirt flung across one end of it. Two pairs of shoes and a pair of slippers were lined up underneath the cot. An old-fashioned dresser stood opposite the cot. A handful of ties dangled raggedly from the bar that had been fastened on its side. A small kitchen table stood in the corner nearest to the kitchen. A box of crackers and a glass, still spotted with milk stains, stood upon the table. A massive desk stood a few feet from the table and the top of it was bare except for an old typewriter and a photograph in a stand-up frame.

Spencer walked over to the desk and began pulling out the drawers. They were almost empty. In one he found a pipe, a box of paper clips, a stapler and a single poker chip. The others yielded other odds and ends, but nothing of importance. In one was a half a ream of paper – but nowhere was there a single line of writing. In the bottom drawer on the left hand side, he found a squat bottle, half full of good Scotch.

And that was all.

He searched the dresser. Nothing but shirts and underwear and socks.

He prowled into the kitchen. Just the built-in stove and refrigerator and the cupboards. He found nothing in any of them but a small supply of food.

And the bedrooms – two of them – were empty, innocent of furniture, and with a fine and powdery dust coating floor and walls. Spencer stood in the doorway of each and looked and there was a sadness in each room. He didn't go inside.

Back in the living room, he went to the desk and picked up the photograph. A woman with a tired, brave smile, with a halo of white hair, with an air of endless patience, looked out of it at him.

There was nothing to be found in this house, he told himself. Not unless one had the time to search every corner of it, every crack, to take it down, each board and stone. And even then, he doubted now, there'd be anything to find.

He left the house and drove back to the office.

'Your lunch didn't take too long,' Miss Crane told him, sourly.

'Everything all right?' he asked.

'The police were very, very nice,' she said. 'Both Mr Hawkes and Mr Snell are anxious to see you. And Mr Garside called.'

'After a while,' said Spencer. 'I've got work to do. I don't want to be disturbed.'

He went into his office and shut the door with a gesture of finality.

From the drawer he took the Hudson papers and settled down to read.

He was no engineer, but he knew enough of it to make a ragged sort of sense, although at times he was forced to go back and read more carefully, or puzzle out a diagram that he'd skipped through too hurriedly. Finally he came to the end of it.

It was all there.

It would have to be checked by technicians and engineers, of course. There might be bugs that would take some ironing out, but the concept, complete both in theory and in the theory's application, was all there in the paper.

Hudson had held nothing back – no vital point, no key.

And that was crazy, Spencer told himself. You had to leave yourself some sort of bargaining position. You could trust no other man, certainly no corporation, as implicitly as Hudson apparently had intended to. Especially you couldn't trust an outfit that had fired you fifteen years before for working on this very concept.

It was ridiculous and tragic, Spencer told himself.

Past, Inc., could not have even guessed what Hudson might have been aiming at. And Hudson, in his turn, was gagged because he'd not as yet progressed to a point where he could have faith either in his concept or himself. Even if he had tried

144

to tell them, they would have laughed at him, for he had no reputation to support such outrageous dreaming.

Spencer sat at his desk, remembering the house on Greenwich Street, the huddling in one room with the other rooms all bare and the entire house stripped of all evidence of comfort and good living. More than likely all the furniture in those rooms, all the accumulation of many years of living, had been sold, piece by precious piece, to keep groceries on the shelf.

A man who was dedicated to a dream, Spencer told himself, a man who had lived with that dream so long and intimately that it was his entire life. Perhaps he had known that he was about to die.

That might explain his impatience at being forced to wait.

Spencer shoved the Hudson papers to one side and picked up the notes. The pages were filled with cryptic pencilled lines, with long strings of mathematical abstractions, roughly drawn sketches. They were no help.

And that other paper, Spencer wondered – the one he'd left in the portfolio, that one that had to do with ethics? Might it not also bear a close relationship to the Hudson concept? Might there not be in it something of importance bearing on this new approach?

Time travel perforce was hedged around with a pattern of ethics which consisted mainly of a formidable list of 'thou shalt nots.'

Thou shalt not transport a human being from the past.

Thou shalt not snitch a thing until it has been lost.

Thou shalt not inform anyone in the past of the fact there is time travel.

Thou shalt not interfere in any way with the patterns of the past.

Thou shalt not try to go into the future – and don't ask why, because that's a dirty question.

VIII

The buzzer sounded. He flipped up the switch.

'Yes, Miss Crane.'

'Mr Garside is here to see you. Mr Hawkes and Mr Snell are with him.'

He thought he detected in her voice a sense of satisfaction.

'All right. Ask them to come in.'

He gathered the papers off his desk and put them in his briefcase, then settled back as they came in. 'Well, gentlemen. It seems I am invaded.'

Even as he said it, he knew it had not been the proper thing to say. They did not even smile. And he knew that it was bad. Any time you got Legal and Public Relations together, it couldn't be anything but bad.

They sat down. 'We thought,' said Snell, in his most polished PR manner, 'that if we got together and tried to talk things out . . .'

Hawkes cut him short. He said to Spencer, accusingly: 'You have managed to place us in a most embarrassing position.'

'Yes, I know,' said Spencer. 'Let's tick off the items. One of my men brought back a human from the past. A man died in my office. I forgot to be polite to a stuffed shirt who came charging in to help us run our business.'

'You seem,' said Garside, 'to take it all quite lightly.'

'Perhaps I do,' said Spencer. 'Let's put it slightly stronger. I just don't give a damn. You cannot allow pressure groups to form your policy.'

'You are talking now, of course,' said Garside, 'about the Ravenholt affair.'

'Chris,' said Snell, enthusiastically, 'you hit it on the button. Here is a chance to really sell the public on us. I don't believe we've really sold them. We are dealing in something which to the average man seems to smell of magic. Naturally he is stand-offish.'

'More to the point,' said Hawkes, impatiently, 'if we turn down this project – this . . .'

'Project God,' said Spencer.

'I'm not sure I like your phrasing.'

'Think up a name yourself,' said Spencer calmly. 'That is what we call it.'

'If we fail to go ahead with it, we'll be accused of being atheists.'

'How would the public ever know that we turned it down?' asked Spencer.

'You can be sure,' Snell said bitterly, 'that Ravenholt will make a point of making known our turning down of it.'

Spencer smashed his fist upon the desk in sudden anger. He yelled, 'I told you how to handle Ravenholt!'

'Hal,' Garside told him quietly, 'we simply cannot do it. We have our dignity.'

'No,' said Spencer, 'I suppose you can't. But you can sell out to Ravenholt and whoever's backing him. You can rig the survey of religious origins. You can falsify reports.'

The three of them sat in stricken silence. Spencer felt a twinge of momentary wonder for having dared to say it. It was not the way one was supposed to talk to brass.

But he had to say one more thing. 'Chris. You are going to disregard the report I made and go ahead with it, aren't you?'

Garside answered with smooth urbanity: 'I'm afraid I'll have to.'

Spencer looked at Hawkes and Snell and he saw the secret smiles that lurked just behind their lips – the sneering contemptuous smile of authority ascendant.

He said slowly, 'Yes, I guess you will. Well, it's all in your laps now. You figure out the answer.'

'But it's your department.'

'Not any more, it isn't. I've just quit the job.'

'Now see here, Hal,' Garside was saying, 'you can't do a thing like that! Without any notice! Just flying off the handle! We may have our little differences, but that is no excuse . . .'

'I've decided,' Spencer told him, 'that I somehow have to stop you. I cannot allow you to go ahead with Project God. I warn you, if you do, that I shall discredit you. I shall prove exactly and without question everything you've done. And meanwhile, I am planning to go into business for myself.'

'Time travel, perhaps.'

They were mocking him.

'I had thought of it.'

Snell grinned contemptuously. 'You can't even get a licence.'

'I think I can,' said Spencer.

And he knew he could. With a brand new concept, there'd be little trouble.

Garside got up from his chair. 'Well,' he said to Spencer, 'you've had your little tantrum. When you cool down a bit, come up and talk to me.'

Spencer shook his head.

'Goodbye, Chris,' he said.

He did not rise. He sat and watched them go.

Strangely, now that it was over – or just beginning – there was no tenseness in him. It had fallen all away and he felt abiding calm.

There was money to be raised, there were technicians and engineers to hire, there were travellers to be found and trained, and a whole lot more than that.

Thinking of it all, he had a momentary pang of doubt, but he shrugged it off. He got up from his chair and walked out into the office.

'Miss Crane,' he said, 'Mr Cabell was supposed to come back this afternoon.'

'I haven't seen him, sir.'

'Of course not,' Spencer said.

For suddenly it all seemed to be coming clear, if he only could believe it.

There had been a look in young Cabell's eyes that had been most disturbing. And now, all at once, he knew that look for exactly what it was.

It had been adulation!

The kind of look that was reserved for someone who had become a legend.

And he must be wrong, Spencer told himself, for he was not a legend – at least not at the moment.

There had been something else in young Cabell's eyes. And once again he knew. Cabell had been a young man, but the eyes had been old eyes. They were eyes that had seen much more of life than a man of thirty had any right to see.

'What shall I say,' asked Miss Crane, 'if he should come back?'

'Never mind,' said Spencer. 'I am sure he won't.'

For Cabell's job was done, if it had been a job at all. It might have been, he told himself, a violation of the ethics, a pure piece of meddling, or it might have been a yielding to that temptation to play God.

Or, he thought, it might have been all planned.

Had they somewhere in the future worked out that formula he'd spoken of to Cabell – the formula that would allow legitimate manipulation of the past?

'Miss Crane,' he said, 'would you be kind enough to type up

a resignation for me? Effective immediately. Make it very formal. I am sore at Garside.'

Miss Crane did not bat an eyelash. She ran paper into her machine.

'Mr Spencer, what reason shall I give?'

'You might say I'm going into business for myself.'

Had there been another time, he wondered, when it hadn't gone this way? Had there been a time when Hudson had gotten in to see him and maybe had not died at all? Had there been a time when he'd handed over the Hudson concept to Past, Inc., instead of stealing it himself?

And if Cabell had not been here to take up the time, more than likely he would have gotten around to seeing Hudson before it was too late. And if he had seen the man, then it was more than likely that he would have passed the concept on through proper channels.

But even so, he wondered, how could they be sure (whoever they might be) that he'd not see Hudson first? He recalled distinctly that Miss Crane had urged that he see him first.

And that was it, he thought excitedly. That was exactly it! He might very well have seen Hudson first if Miss Crane had not been insistent that he should.

And standing there, he thought of all the years that Miss Crane must have worked at it – conditioning him to the point where he'd be sure to do exactly opposite to what she urged he do.

'Mr Spencer,' said Miss Crane, 'I have the letter finished. And there is something else. I almost forgot about it.'

She reached down into a drawer and took out something and laid it on the desk.

It was the portfolio that belonged to Hudson.

'The police,' said Miss Crane, 'apparently overlooked it. It was very careless of them. I thought that you might like it.'

Spencer stood staring blankly at it.

'It would go so nicely,' said Miss Crane, 'with the other stuff you have.'

There was a muted thumping on the floor and Spencer spun around. A white rabbit with long and droopy ears hopped across the carpet, looking for a carrot.

'Oh, how cute!' cried Miss Crane, very much unlike herself. 'Is it the one that Mr Nickerson sent back?'

'It's the one,' said Spencer. 'I had forgotten it.'

'Might I have it?'

'Miss Crane, I wonder . . .'

'Yes, Mr Spencer?'

And what was he to say?

Could he blurt out that now he knew she was one of them?

It would take so much explanation and it could be so involved. And, besides, Miss Crane was not the sort of person that you blurted out things to.

He gulped. 'I was wondering, Miss Crane, if you'd come and work for me. I'll need a secretary.'

Miss Crane shook her head. 'No, I'm getting old. I'm thinking of retiring. I think, now that you are leaving, I shall just disappear.'

'But, Miss Crane, I'll need you desperately.'

'One of these days soon,' said Miss Crane, 'when you need a secretary, there'll be an applicant. She'll wear a bright green dress and she'll be wearing these new glasses and be carrying a snow-white rabbit with a bow around its neck. She may strike you as something of a hussy, but you hire her. Be sure you hire her.'

'I'll remember,' Spencer said. 'I'll be looking for her. I'll hire no one else.'

'She will not,' warned Miss Crane, 'be a bit like me. She'll be much nicer.'

'Thank you, Miss Crane,' said Spencer, just a bit inanely.

'And don't forget this,' said Miss Crane, holding out the portfolio.

He took it and headed for the door.

At the door he stopped and turned back to her.

'I'll be seeing you,' he said.

For the first time in fifteen years, Miss Crane smiled at him.

THE AUTUMN LAND

He sat on the porch in the rocking chair, with the loose board creaking as he rocked. Across the street the old white-haired lady cut a bouquet of chrysanthemums in the never-ending autumn. Where he could see between the ancient houses to the distant woods and wastelands, a soft Indian summer blue lay upon the land. The entire village was soft and quiet, as old things often are – a place constructed for a dreaming mind rather than a living being. It was an hour too early for his other old and shaky neighbour to come fumbling down the grass-grown sidewalk, tapping the bricks with his seeking cane. And he would not hear the distant children at their play until dusk had fallen – if he heard them then. He did not always hear them.

There were books to read, but he did not want to read them. He could go into the backyard and spade and rake the garden once again, reducing the soil to a finer texture to receive the seed when it could be planted – if it ever could be planted – but there was slight incentive in the further preparation of a seed bed against a spring that never came. Earlier, much earlier, before he knew about the autumn and the spring, he had mentioned garden seeds to the Milkman, who had been very much embarrassed.

He had walked the magic miles and left the world behind in bitterness and when he first had come here had been content to live in utter idleness, to be supremely idle and to feel no guilt or shame at doing absolutely nothing or as close to absolutely nothing as a man was able. He had come walking down the autumn street in the quietness and the golden sunshine, and the first person that he saw was the old lady who lived across the street. She had been waiting at the gate of her picket fence as if she had known he would be coming, and she had said to him, 'You're a new one come to live with us. There are not many come these days. That is your house across the street from me, and I know we'll be good neighbours.' He had reached up his hand to doff his hat to her, forgetting that he had no hat. 'My name is Nelson Rand,' he'd told her. 'I am an engineer. I will try to be a decent neighbour.' He had the impression that she stood taller and straighter than she did, but old and bent as she might be there was a comforting graciousness about her. 'You will please come in,' she said. 'I have lemonade and cookies. There are other people there, but I shall not introduce them to you.' He waited for her to explain why she would not introduce him, but there was no explanation, and he followed her down the time-mellowed walk of bricks with great beds of asters and chrysanthemums, a mass of colour on either side of it.

In the large, high-ceilinged living room, with its bay windows forming window seats, filled with massive furniture from another time and with a small blaze burning in the fireplace, she had shown him to a seat before a small table to one side of the fire and had sat down opposite him and poured the lemonade and passed the plate of cookies.

'You must pay no attention to them,' she had told him. 'They are all dying to meet you, but I shall not humour them.'

It was easy to pay no attention to them, for there was no one there.

'The Major, standing over there by the fireplace,' said his hostess, 'with the elbow on the mantel, a most ungainly pose if you should ask me, is not happy with my lemonade. He would prefer a stronger drink. Please, Mr Rand, will you not taste my lemonade? I assure you it is good. I made it myself. I have no maid, you see, and no one in the kitchen. I live quite by myself and satisfactorily, although my friends keep dropping in, sometimes more often than I like.'

He tasted the lemonade, not without misgivings, and to his surprise it was lemonade and was really good, like the lemonade he had drunk when a boy at Fourth of July celebrations and at grade school picnics, and had never tasted since.

152

'It is excellent,' he said.

'The lady in blue,' his hostess said, 'sitting in the chair by the window, lived here many years ago. She and I were friends, although she moved away some time ago and I am surprised that she comes back, which she often does. The infuriating thing is that I cannot remember her name, if I ever knew it. You don't know it, do you?'

'I am afraid I don't.'

'Oh, of course, you wouldn't. I had forgotten. I forget so easily these days. You are a new arrival.'

He had sat through the afternoon and drank her lemonade and eaten her cookies, while she chattered on about her nonexistent guests. It was only when he had crossed the street to the house she had pointed out as his, with her standing on the stoop and waving her farewell, that he realized she had not told him her name. He did not know it even now.

How long had it been? he wondered, and realized he didn't know. It was this autumn business. How could a man keep track of time when it was always autumn?

It all had started on that day when he'd been driving across Iowa, heading for Chicago. No, he reminded himself, it had started with the thinnesses, although he had paid little attention to the thinnesses to begin with. Just been aware of them, perhaps as a strange condition of the mind, or perhaps an unusual quality to the atmosphere and light. As if the world lacked a certain solidity that one had come to expect, as if one were running along a mystic borderline between here and somewhere else.

He had lost his West Coast job when a government contract had failed to materialize. His company had not been the only one; there were many other companies that were losing contracts and there were a lot of engineers who walked the streets bewildered. There was a bare possibility of a job in Chicago, although he was well aware that by now it might be filled. Even if there were no job, he reminded himself, he was in better shape than a lot of other men. He was young and single, he had a few dollars in the bank, he had no house mortgage, no car payments, no kids to put through school. He had only himself to support – no family of any sort at all. The old, hard-fisted bachelor uncle who had taken him to raise when his parents had died in a car crash and had worked him

153

hard on that stony, hilly Wisconsin farm, had receded deep into the past, becoming a dim, far figure that was hard to recognize. He had not liked his uncle, Rand remembered – had not hated him, simply had not liked him. He had shed no tears, he recalled, when the old man had been caught out in a pasture by a bull and gored to death. So now Rand was quite alone, not even holding the memories of a family.

He had been hoarding the little money that he had, for with a limited work record, with other men better qualified looking for the jobs, he realized that it might be some time before he could connect with anything. The beat-up waggon that he drove had space for sleeping, and he stopped at the little wayside parks along the way to cook his meals.

He had almost crossed the state, and the road had started its long winding through the bluffs that rimmed the Mississippi. Ahead he caught a glimpse, at several turnings of the road, of smokestacks and tall structures that marked the city just ahead.

He emerged from the bluffs, and the city was before him, a small industrial centre that lay on either side of the river. It was then that he felt and saw (if one could call it seeing) the thinness that he had seen before or had sensed before. There was about it, not exactly an alienness, but a sense of unreality, as if one were seeing the actuality of the scene through some sort of veil, with the edges softened and the angles flattened out, as if one might be looking at it as one would look at the bottom of a clear-water lake with a breeze gently ruffling the surface. When he had seen it before, he had attributed it to road fatigue and had opened the window to get a breath of air or had stopped the car and gotten out to walk up and down the road a while, and it had gone away.

But this time it was worse than ever, and he was somewhat frightened at it – not so much frightened at it as he was frightened of himself, wondering what might be wrong with him.

He pulled off to the side of the road, braking the car to a halt, and it seemed to him, even as he did it, that the shoulder of the road was rougher than he'd thought. As he pulled off the road, the thinness seemed to lessen, and he saw that the road had changed, which explained its roughness. The surface was pocked with chuckholes and blocks of concrete had been heaved up and other blocks were broken into pebbly shards.

154

He raised his eyes from the road to look at the city, and there was no city, only the broken stumps of a place that had somehow been destroyed. He sat with his hands frozen on the wheel, and in the silence – the deadly, unaccustomed silence – he heard the cawing of crows. Foolishly, he tried to remember the last time he had heard the caw of crows, and then he saw them, black specks that flapped just above the bluff top. There was something else as well – the trees. No longer trees, but only here and there blackened stumps. The stumps of a city and the stumps of trees, with the black, ash-like flecks of crows flapping over them.

Scarcely knowing what he did, he stumbled from the car. Thinking of it later, it had seemed a foolish thing to do, for the car was the only thing he knew, the one last link he had to reality. As he stumbled from it, he put his hand down in the seat, and beneath his hand he felt the solid, oblong object. His fingers closed upon it, and it was not until he was standing by the car that he realized what he held – the camera that had been lying in the seat beside him.

Sitting on the porch, with the loose floor board creaking underneath the rocker, he remembered that he still had the pictures, although it had been a long time since he had thought of them – a long life, actually, since he'd thought of anything at all beyond his life, day to day, in this autumn land. It was as though he had been trying to keep himself from thinking, attempting to keep his mind in neutral, to shut out what he knew – or, more precisely perhaps, what he thought he knew.

He did not consciously take the pictures, although afterward he had tried to tell himself he did (but never quite convincing himself that this was entirely true), complimenting himself in a wry sort of way for providing a piece of evidence that his memory alone never could have provided. For a man can think so many things, daydream so many things, imagine so many things that he can never trust his mind.

The entire incident, when he later thought of it, was hazy, as if the reality of that blasted city lay in some strange dimension of experience that could not be explained, or even rationalized. He could remember only vaguely the camera at his eyes and the clicking as the shutter snapped. He did recall the band of people charging down the hill toward him and his mad scramble for the car, locking the door behind him and putting the car in gear, intent on steering a zigzag course along the broken pavement to get away from the screaming humans who were less than a hundred feet away.

But as he pulled off the shoulder, the pavement was no longer broken. It ran smooth and level toward the city that was no longer blasted. He pulled off the road again and sat limply, beaten, and it was only after many minutes that he could proceed again, going very slowly because he did not trust himself, shaken as he was, to drive at greater speed.

He had planned to cross the river and continue to Chicago, getting there that night, but now his plans were changed. He was too shaken up and, besides, there were the films. And he needed time to think, he told himself, a lot of time to think.

He found a roadside park a few miles outside the city and pulled into it, parking alongside an outdoor grill and an old-fashioned pump. He got some wood from the small supply he carried in the back and built a fire. He hauled out the box with his cooking gear and food, fixed the coffee pot, set a pan upon the grill and cracked three eggs into it.

When he had pulled off the road, he had seen the man walking along the roadside; and now, as he cracked the eggs, he saw that the man had turned into the park and was walking toward the car. The man came up to the pump.

'Does this thing work?' he asked.

Rand nodded. 'I got water for the pot,' he said. 'Just now.'

'It's a hot day,' said the man.

He worked the pump handle up and down.

'Hot for walking,' he said.

'You been walking far?'

'The last six weeks,' he said.

Rand had a closer look at him. The clothes were old and worn, but fairly clean. He had shaved a day or two before. His hair was long – not that he wore it long, but from lack of barbering.

Water gushed from the spout and the man cupped his hands under it, bent to drink.

'That was good,' he finally said. 'I was thirsty.'

'How are you doing for food?' asked Rand.

The man hesitated. 'Not too well,' he said.

'Reach into that box on the tailgate. Find yourself a plate
156

and some eating implements. A cup, too. Coffee will be ready soon.'

'Mister, I wouldn't want you to think I was walking up here . . .'

'Forget it,' said Rand. 'I know how it is. There's enough for both of us.'

The man got a plate and cup, a knife, a fork, a spoon. He came over and stood beside the fire.

'I am new at this,' he said. 'I've never had to do a thing like this before. I always had a job. For seventeen years I had a job . . .'

'Here you are,' said Rand. He slid the eggs onto the plate, went back to the box to get three more.

The man walked over to a picnic table and put down his plate. 'Don't wait for me,' said Rand. 'Eat them while they're hot. The coffee's almost ready. There's bread if you want any.'

'I'll get a slice later,' said the man, 'for mopping up.'

John Sterling, he said his name was, and where now would John Sterling be, Rand wondered – still tramping the highways, looking for work, any kind of work, a day of work, an hour of work, a man who for seventeen years had held a job and had a job no longer? Thinking of Sterling, he felt a pang of guilt. He owed John Sterling a debt he never could repay, not knowing at the time they talked there was any debt involved.

They had sat and talked, eating their eggs, mopping up the plates with bread, drinking hot coffee.

'For seventeen years,' said Sterling. 'A machine operator. An experienced hand. With the same company. Then they let me out. Me and four hundred others. All at one time. Later they let out others. I was not the only one. There were a lot of us. We weren't laid off, we were let out. No promise of going back. Not the company's fault, I guess. There was a big contract that fizzled out. There was no work to do. How about yourself? You let out, too?'

Rand nodded. 'How did you know?'

'Well, eating like this. Cheaper than a restaurant. And you got a sleeping bag. You sleep in the car?'

'That is right,' said Rand. 'It's not as bad for me as it is for some of the others. I have no family.'

'I have a family,' said Sterling. 'Wife, three kids. We talked it over, the wife and me. She didn't want me to leave, but it

157

made sense I should. Money all gone, unemployment run out. Long as I was around, it was hard to get relief. But if I deserted her, she could get relief. That way there's food for the wife and kids, a roof over their heads. Hardest thing I ever did. Hard for all of us. Someday I'll go back. When times get better, I'll go back. The family will be waiting.'

Out on the highway the cars went whisking past. A squirrel came down out of a tree, advanced cautiously toward the table, suddenly turned and fled for his very life, swarming up a nearby trunk.

'I don't know,' said Sterling. 'It might be too big for us, this society of ours. It may be out of hand. I read a lot. Always liked to read. And I think about what I read. It seems to me maybe we've outrun our brains. The brains we have maybe were OK back in prehistoric days. We did all right with the brains we had until we built too big and complex. Maybe we built beyond our brains. Maybe our brains no longer are good enough to handle what we have. We have set loose economic forces we don't understand and political forces that we do not understand, and if we can't understand them, we can't control them. Maybe that is why you and I are out of jobs.'

'I wouldn't know,' said Rand. 'I never thought about it.'

'A man thinks a lot,' said Sterling. 'He dreams a lot walking down the road. Nothing else to do. He dreams some silly things: things that are silly on the face of them, but are hard to say can't be really true. Did this ever happen to you?'

'Sometimes,' said Rand.

'One thing I thought about a lot. A terribly silly thought. Maybe thinking it because I do so much walking. Sometimes people pick me up, but mostly I walk. And I got to wondering if a man should walk far enough could he leave it all behind? The farther a man might walk, the farther he would be from everything.'

'Where you heading?' Rand asked.

'Nowhere in particular. Just keep in moving, that is all. Month or so I'll start heading south. Get a good head start on winter. These northern states are no place to be when winter comes.'

'There are two eggs left,' said Rand., 'How about it?'

'Hell, man, I can't. I already . . .'

'Three eggs aren't a lot. I can get some more.'

158

'Well, if you're sure that you don't mind. Tell you what — let's split them, one for you, one for me.'

The giddy old lady had finished cutting her bouquet and had gone into the house. From up the street came the tapping of a cane — Rand's other ancient neighbour, out for his evening walk. The sinking sun poured a blessing on the land. The leaves were gold and red, brown and yellow — they had been that way since the day that Rand had come. The grass had a tawny look about it — not dead, just dressed up for dying.

The old man came trudging carefully down the walk, his cane alert against a stumble, helping himself with it without really needing any help. He was slow, was all. He halted by the walk that ran up to the porch. 'Good afternoon,' he said. 'Good afternoon,' said Rand. 'You have a nice day for your walk.' The old man acknowledged the observation graciously and with a touch of modesty, as if he, himself, might somehow be responsible for the goodness of the day. 'It looks,' he said, 'as if we might have another fine day tomorrow.' And having said that, he continued down the street.

It was ritual. The same words were said every day. The situation, like the village and the weather, never varied. He could sit here on this porch a thousand years, Rand told himself, and the old man would continue going past and each time the selfsame words would be mouthed — a set piece, a strip of film run over and over again. Something here had happened to time. The year had stuck on autumn.

Rand did not understand it. He did not try to understand it. There was no way for him to try. Sterling had said that man's cleverness might have outstripped his feeble prehistoric mind — or, perhaps, his brutal and prehistoric mind. And here there was less chance of understanding than there had been back in that other world.

He found himself thinking of that other world in the same myth-haunted way as he thought of this one. The one now seemed as unreal as the other. Would he ever, Rand wondered, find reality again? Did he want to find it?

There was a way to find reality, he knew. Go into the house and take out the photos in the drawer of his bedside table and have a look at them. Refresh his memory, stare reality in the face again. For those photos, grim as they might be, were a harder reality than this world in which he sat or the world that

159

he had known. For they were nothing seen by the human eye, interpreted by the human brain. They were, somehow, fact. The camera saw what it saw and could not lie about it; it did not fantasize, it did not rationalize, and it had no faulty memory, which was more than could be said of the human mind.

He had gone back to the camera shop where he had left the film and the clerk had picked out the envelope from the box behind the counter.

'That will be three ninety-five,' he said.

Rand took a five-dollar bill out of his wallet and laid it on the counter.

'If you don't mind my asking,' said the clerk, 'where did you get these pictures?'

'It is trick photography,' said Rand.

The clerk shook his head. 'If that is what they are, they're the best I've ever seen.'

The clerk rang up the sale and, leaving the register open, stepped back and picked up the envelope.

'What do you want?' asked Rand.

The man shook the prints out of the envelope, shuffled through them.

'This one,' he said.

Rand stared at him levelly. 'What about it?' he asked.

'The people. I know some of them. The one in front. That is Bob Gentry. He is my best friend.'

'You must be mistaken,' Rand said coldly.

He took the prints from the clerk's fingers, put them back in the envelope.

The clerk made the change. He still was shaking his head, confused, perhaps a little frightened, when Rand left the shop.

He drove carefully, but with no loss of time, through the city and across the bridge. When he hit open country beyond the river, he built up his speed, keeping an eye on the rear-vision mirror. The clerk had been upset, perhaps enough to phone the police. Others would have seen the pictures and been upset as well. Although, he told himself, it was silly to think of the police. In taking the photos, he had broken no regulations, violated no laws. He had had a perfect right to take them.

Across the river and twenty miles down the highway, he turned off into a small, dusty country road and followed it until

160

he found a place to pull off, where the road widened at the approach to a bridge that crossed a small stream. There was evidence that the pull-off was much used, fishermen more than likely parking their cars there while they tried their luck. But now the place was empty.

He was disturbed to find that his hands were shaking when he pulled the envelope from his pocket and shook out the prints.

And there it was — as he no longer could remember it.

He was surprised that he had taken as many pictures as he had. He could not remember having taken half that many. But they were there, and as he looked at them, his memory, reinforced, came back again, although the photos were much sharper than his memory. The world, he recalled, had seemed to be hazed and indistinct as far as his eyes had been concerned; in the photos it lay cruel and merciless and clear. The blackened stumps stood up, stark and desolate, and there could be no doubt that the imprint that lay upon the photos was the actuality of a bombed-out city. The photos of the bluff showed the barren rock no longer masked by trees, with only here and there the skeletons of trees that by some accidental miracle had not been utterly reduced by the storm of fire. There was only one photo of the band of people who had come charging down the hill toward him; and that was understandable, for once having seen them, he had been in a hurry to get back to the car. Studying the photo, he saw they were much closer than he'd thought. Apparently they had been there all the time, just a little way off, and he had not noticed them in his astonishment at what had happened to the city. If they had been quieter about it, they could have been on top of him and overwhelmed him before he discovered them. He looked closely at the picture and saw that they had been close enough that some of the faces were fairly well defined. He wondered which one of them was the man the clerk back at the camera shop had recognized.

He shuffled the photographs together and slid them back into the envelope and put it in his pocket. He got out of the car and walked down to the edge of the stream. The stream, he saw, was no more than ten feet or so across; but here, below the bridge, it had gathered itself into a pool, and the bank had been trampled bare of vegetation, and there were places where

161

fishermen had sat. Rand sat down in one of these places and inspected the pool. The current came in close against the bank and probably had undercut it, and lying there, in the undercut, would be the fish that the now-absent anglers sought, dangling their worms at the end of a long cane pole and waiting for a bite.

The place was pleasant and cool, shaded by a great oak that grew on the bank just below the bridge. From some far-off field came the subdued clatter of a mower. The water dimpled as a fish came up to suck in a floating insect. A good place to stay, thought Rand. A place to sit and rest awhile. He tried to blank his mind, to wipe out the memory and the photos, to pretend that nothing at all had happened, that there was nothing he must think about.

But there was, he found, something that he must think about. Not about the photos, but something that Sterling had said just the day before. 'I got to wondering,' he had said, 'if a man should walk far enough, could he leave it all behind.'

How desperate must a man get, Rand wondered, before he would be driven to asking such a question. Perhaps not desperate at all – just worried and alone and tired and not being able to see the end of it. Either that, or afraid of what lay up ahead. Like knowing, perhaps, that in a few years' time (and not too many years, for in that photo of the people the clerk had seen a man he knew) a warhead would hit a little Iowa town and wipe it out. Not that there was any reason for it being hit; it was no Los Angeles, no New York, no Washington, no busy port, no centre of transportation or communication, held no great industrial complex, was no seat of government. Simply hit because it had been there, hit by blunder, by malfunction, or by miscalculation. Although it probably didn't matter greatly, for by the time it had been hit, the nation and perhaps the world might have been gone. A few years, Rand told himself, and it would come to that. After all the labour, all the hopes and dreams, the world would come to just that.

It was the sort of thing that a man might want to walk away from, hoping that in time he might forget it ever had been there. But to walk away, he thought, rather idly, one would have to find a starting point. You could not walk away from everything by just starting anywhere.

It was an idle thought, sparked by the memory of his talk

162

with Sterling; and he sat there, idly, on the stream bank; and because it had a sense of attractive wonder, he held it in his mind, not letting go at once as one did with idle thoughts. And as he sat there, still holding it in mind, another thought, another time and place crept in to keep it company; and suddenly he knew, with no doubt at all, without really thinking, without searching for an answer, that he knew the place where he could start.

He stiffened and sat rigid, momentarily frightened, feeling like a fool trapped by his own unconscious fantasy. For that, said common sense, was all that it could be. The bitter wondering of a beaten man as he tramped the endless road looking for a job, the shock of what the photos showed, some strange, mesmeric quality of this shaded pool that seemed a place apart from a rock-hard world – all of these put together had produced the fantasy.

Rand hauled himself erect and turned back toward the car, but as he did he could see within his mind this special starting place. He had been a boy – how old? he wondered, maybe nine or ten – and he had found the little valley (not quite a glen, yet not quite a valley, either) running below his uncle's farm down toward the river. He had never been there before and he had never gone again; on his uncle's farm there had been too many chores, too many things to do to allow the time to go anywhere at all. He tried to recall the circumstances of his being there and found that he could not. All that he could remember was a single magic moment, as if he had been looking at a single frame of a movie film – a single frame impressed upon his memory because of what? Because of some peculiar angle at which the light had struck the landscape? Because for an instant he had seen with different eyes than he'd ever used before or since? Because for the fractional part of a second he had sensed a simple truth behind the facade of the ordinary world? No matter what, he knew, he had seen magic in that moment.

He went back to the car and sat behind the wheel, staring at the bridge and sliding water and the field beyond, but seeing, instead of them, the map inside his head. When he went back to the highway, he'd turn left instead of right, back toward the river and the town, and before he reached them he would turn north on another road and the valley of the magic moment would be only a little more than a hundred miles away. He sat and saw the map and purpose hardened in his mind. Enough of this silliness, he thought; there were no magic moments, never had been one; when he reached the highway, he'd turn to the right and hope the job might still be there when he reached Chicago.

When he reached the highway, he turned not right, but left.

It had been so easy to find, he thought as he sat on the porch. There had been no taking of wrong roads, no stopping for directions; he'd gone directly there as if he'd always known he would be coming back and had kept the way in mind. He had parked the car at the hollow's mouth, since there was no road, and had gone on foot up the little valley. It could so easily have been that he would not have found the place, he told himself, admitting now for the first time since it all began that he might not have been so sure as he had thought he was. He might have gone up the full length of the valley and not have found the magic ground, or he might have passed it by, seeing it with other eyes and not recognizing it.

But it still was there, and he had stopped and looked at it and known it; again he was only nine or ten, and it was all right, the magic still was there. He had found a path he had not seen before and had followed it, the magic still remaining; and when he reached the hilltop, the village had been there. He had walked down the street in the quietness of the golden sunshine, and the first person that he had seen had been the old lady waiting at the gate of her picket fence, as if she had been told that he would be coming.

After he had left her house he went across the street to the house she said was his. As he came in the front door, there was someone knocking at the back.

'I am the Milkman,' the knocker had explained. He was a shadowy sort of person; you could see and yet you did not really see him; when one looked away and then looked back at him, it was as if one were seeing someone he had never seen before.

'Milkman,' Rand had said. 'Yes, I suppose I could do with milk.'

'Also,' said the Milkman, 'I have eggs, bread, butter, bacon and other things that you will need. Here is a can of oil; you'll need it for your lamps. The woodshed is well stocked, and when there's need of it, I'll replenish it. The kindling's to the left as you go through the door.'

Rand recalled that he'd never paid the Milkman or even mentioned payment. The Milkman was not the kind of man to whom one mentioned money. There was no need, either, to leave an order slip in the milkbox; the Milkman seemed to know what one might need and when without being told. With some shame, Rand remembered the time he had mentioned garden seeds and caused embarrassment, not only for the Milkman, but for himself as well. For as soon as he mentioned them, he had sensed that he'd broken some very subtle code of which he should have been aware.

The day was fading into evening, and he should be going in soon to cook himself a meal. And after that, what, he wondered. There still were books to read, but he did not want to read them. He could take out from the desk the plan he had laid out for the garden and mull over it a while, but now he knew he'd never plant the garden. You didn't plant a garden in a forever-autumn land, and there were no seeds.

Across the street a light blossomed in the windows of that great front room with its massive furniture, its roomy window seats, the great fireplace flaring to the ceiling. The old man with the cane had not returned, and it was getting late for him. In the distance now Rand could hear the sounds of children playing in the dusk.

The old and young, he thought. The old, who do not care; the young, who do not think. And what was he doing here, neither young nor old?

He left the porch and went down the walk. The street was empty, as it always was. He drifted slowly down it, heading toward the little park at the village edge. He often went there, to sit on a bench beneath the friendly trees; and it was there, he was sure, that he would find the children. Although why he should think that he would find them there he did not know, for he had never found them, but only heard their voices.

He went past the houses, standing sedately in the dusk. Had people ever lived in them, he wondered. Had there ever been that many people in this nameless village? The old lady across the street spoke of friends she once had known, of people who had lived here and had gone away. But was this her memory speaking or the kind befuddlement of someone growing old?

The houses, he had noted, all were in good repair. A loose shingle here and there, a little peeling paint, but no windows broken, no loosened gutters, sagging from the eaves, no rotting porch posts. As if, he thought, good householders had been here until very recently.

He reached the park and could see that it was empty. He still heard the childish voices, crying at their play, but they had receded and now came from somewhere just beyond the park. He crossed the park and stood at its edge, staring off across the scrub and abandoned fields.

In the east the moon was rising, a full moon that lighted the landscape so that he could see every little clump of bushes, every grove of trees. And as he stood there, he realized with a sudden start that the moon was full again, that it was always full. It rose with the setting of the sun and set just before the sun came up, and it was always a great pumpkin of a moon, an eternal harvest moon shining on an eternal autumn world.

The realization that this was so all at once seemed shocking. How was it that he had never noticed this before? Certainly he had been here long enough, had watched the moon often enough to have noticed it. He had been here long enough – and how long had that been, a few weeks, a few months, a year? He found he did not know. He tried to figure back and there was no way to figure back. There were no temporal landmarks. Nothing ever happened to mark one day from the next. Time flowed so smoothly and so uneventfully that it might as well stand still.

The voices of the playing children had been moving from him, becoming fainter in the distance; and as he listened to them, he found that he was hearing them in his mind when they were no longer there. They had come and played and now had ceased their play. They would come again, if not tomorrow night, in another night or two. It did not matter, he admitted, if they came or not, for they really weren't there.

He turned heavily about and went back through the streets. As he approached his house, a dark figure moved out from the shadow of the trees and stood waiting for him. It was the old lady from across the street. It was evident that she had been awaiting his return.

166

'Good evening, ma'am,' he said gravely. 'It is a pleasant night.'

'He is gone,' she said. 'He did not come back. He went just like the others and he won't come back.'

'You mean the old man.'

'Our neighbour,' she said. 'The old man with the cane. I do not know his name. I never knew his name. And I don't know yours.'

'I told it to you once,' said Rand, but she paid him no attention.

'Just a few doors up the street,' she said, 'and I never knew his name and I doubt that he knew mine. We are a nameless people here, and it is a terrible thing to be a nameless person.'

'I will look for him,' said Rand. 'He may have lost his way.'

'Yes, go and look for him,' she said. 'By all means look for him. It will ease your mind. It will take away the guilt. But you will never find him.'

He took the direction that he knew the old man always took. He had the impression that his ancient neighbour, on his daily walks, went to the town square and the deserted business section, but he did not know. At no other time had it ever seemed important where he might have gone on his walks.

When he emerged into the square, he saw, immediately, the dark object lying on the pavement and recognized it as the old man's hat. There was no sign of the old man himself.

Rand walked out into the square and picked up the hat. He gently reshaped and creased it and after that was done held it carefully by the brim so that it would come to no further damage.

The business section drowsed in the moonlight. The statue of the unknown man stood starkly on its base in the centre of the square. When he first had come here, Rand recalled, he had tried to unravel the identity of the statue and had failed. There was no legend carved into the granite base, no bronze plate affixed. The face was undistinguished, the stony costume gave no hint as to identity or period. There was nothing in the posture or the attitude of the carven body to provide a clue. The statue stood, a forgotten tribute to some unknown mediocrity.

As he gazed about the square at the business houses, Rand was struck again, as he always was, by the carefully unmodern make-up of the establishments. A barber shop, a hotel, a livery barn, a bicycle shop, a harness shop, a grocery store, a meat market, a blacksmith shop – no garage, no service station, no pizza parlour, no hamburger joint. The houses along the quiet streets told the story; here it was emphasized. This was an old town, forgotten and by-passed by the sweep of time, a place of another century. But there was about it all what seemed to be a disturbing sense of unreality, as if it were no old town at all, but a place deliberately fashioned in such a manner as to represent a segment of the past.

Rand shook his head. What was wrong with him tonight? Most of the time he was quite willing to accept the village for what it seemed to be, but tonight he was assailed with uneasy doubt.

Across the square he found the old man's cane. If his neighbour had come in this direction, he reasoned, he must have crossed the square and gone on down the street nearest to the place where he had dropped the cane. But why had he dropped the cane? First his hat and then his cane. What had happened here?

Rand glanced around, expecting that he might catch some movement, some furtive lurker on the margin of the square. There was nothing. If there had been something earlier, there was nothing now.

Following the street toward which his neighbour might have been heading, he walked carefully and alert, watching the shadows closely. The shadows played tricks on him, conjuring up lumpy objects that could have been a fallen man, but weren't. A half a dozen times he froze when he thought he detected something moving, but it was, in each case, only an illusion of the shadows.

When the village ended, the street continued as a path. Rand hesitated, trying to plan his action. The old man had lost his hat and cane, and the points where he had dropped them argued that he had intended going down the street that Rand had followed. If he had come down the street, he might have continued down the path, out of the village and away from it, perhaps fleeing from something in the village.

There was no way one could be sure, Rand knew. But he was here and might as well go on for at least a ways. The old

168

man might be out there somewhere, exhausted, perhaps terribly frightened, perhaps fallen beside the path and needing help.

Rand forged ahead. The path, rather well-defined at first, became fainter as it wound its way across the rolling moonlit countryside. A flushed rabbit went bobbing through the grass. Far off an owl chortled wickedly. A faint chill wind came out of the west. And with the wind came a sense of loneliness, of open empty space untenanted by anything other than rabbit, owl and wind.

The path came to an end, its faintness finally pinching out to nothing. The groves of trees and thickets of low-growing shrubs gave way to a level plain of blowing grass, bleached to whiteness by the moon, a faceless prairie land. Staring out across it, Rand knew that this wilderness of grass would run on and on forever. It had in it the scent and taste of foreverness. He shuddered at the sight of it and wondered why a man should shudder at a thing so simple. But even as he wondered, he knew – the grass was staring back at him; it knew him and waited patiently for him, for in time he would come to it. He would wander into it and be lost in it, swallowed by its immensity and anonymity.

He turned and ran, unashamedly, chill of blood and brain, shaken to the core. When he reached the outskirts of the village, he finally stopped the running and turned to look back into the wasteland. He had left the grass behind, but he sensed illogically that it was stalking him, flowing forward, still out of sight, but soon to appear, with the wind blowing billows in its whiteness.

He ran again, but not so fast and hard this time, jogging down the street. He came into the square and crossed it, and when he reached his house, he saw that the house across the street was dark. He did not hesitate, but went on down the street he'd walked when he first came to the village. For he knew now that he must leave this magic place with its strange and quiet old village, its forever autumn and eternal harvest moon, its faceless sea of grass, its children who receded in the distance when one went to look for them, its old man who walked into oblivion, dropping hat and cane – that he must somehow find his way back to that other world where few jobs existed and men walked the road to find them, where nasty little wars flared in forgotten corners and a camera caught on a film the doom that was to come.

He left the village behind him and knew that he had not far to go to reach the place where the path swerved to the right and down a broken slope into the little valley to the magic starting point he'd found again after many years. He went slowly and carefully so that he would not wander off the path, for as he remembered it the path was very faint. It took much longer than he had thought to reach the point where the path swerved to the right into the broken ground, and the realization grew upon him that the path did not swing to right and there was no broken ground.

In front of him he saw the grass again and there was no path leading into it. He knew that he was trapped, that he would never leave the village until he left it as the old man had, walking out of it and into nothingness. He did not move closer to the grass, for he knew there was terror there and he'd had enough of terror. You're a coward, he told himself.

Retracing the path back to the village, he kept a sharp lookout, going slowly so that he'd not miss the turn off if it should be there. It was not, however. It once had been, he told himself, bemused, and he'd come walking up it, out of that other world he'd fled.

The village street was dappled by the moonlight shining through the rustling leaves. The house across the street still was dark, and there was an empty loneliness about it. Rand remembered that he had not eaten since the sandwich he had made that noon. There'd be something in the milkbox — he'd not looked in it that morning, or had he? He could not remember.

He went around the house to the back porch where the milkbox stood. The Milkman was standing there. He was more shadowy than ever, less well defined, with the moonlight shining on him, and his face was deeply shaded by the wide-brimmed hat he wore.

Rand halted abruptly and stood looking at him, astounded that the Milkman should be there. For he was out of place in the autumn moonlight. He was a creature of the early morning hours and of no other times.

'I came,' the Milkman said, 'to determine if I could be of help.'

170

Rand said nothing. His head buzzed large and misty, and there was nothing to be said.

'A gun,' the Milkman suggested. 'Perhaps you would like a gun.'

'A gun? Why should I want one?'

'You have had a most disturbing evening. You might feel safer, more secure, with a gun in hand, a gun strapped about your waist.'

Rand hesitated. Was there mockery in the Milkman's voice?

'Or a cross.'

'A cross?'

'A crucifix. A symbol . . .'

'No,' said Rand. 'I do not need a cross.'

'A volume of philosophy, perhaps.'

'No!' Rand shouted at him. 'I left all that behind. We tried to use them all, we relied on them and they weren't good enough and now . . .'

He stopped, for that had not been what he'd meant to say, if in fact he'd meant to say anything at all. It was something that he'd never even thought about; it was as if someone inside of him were speaking through his mouth.

'Or perhaps some currency?'

'You are making fun of me,' Rand said bitterly, 'and you have no right . . .'

'I merely mention certain things,' the Milkman said, 'upon which humans place reliance . . .'

'Tell me one thing,' said Rand, 'as simply as you can. Is there any way of going back?'

'Back to where you came from?'

'Yes,' said Rand. 'That is what I mean.'

'There is nothing to go back to,' the Milkman said. 'Anyone who comes has nothing to go back to.'

'But the old man left. He wore a black felt hat and carried a cane. He dropped them and I found them.'

'He did not go back,' the Milkman said. 'He went ahead. And do not ask me where, for I do not know.'

'But you're a part of this.'

'I am a humble servant. I have a job to do and I try to do it well. I care for our guests the best that I am able. But there comes a time when each of our guests leaves us. I would suspect this is a halfway house on the road to someplace else.'

'A place for getting ready,' Rand said.

'What do you mean?' the Milkman asked.

'I am not sure,' said Rand. 'I had not meant to say it.' And this was the second time, he thought, that he'd said something he had not meant to say.

'There's one comfort about this place,' the Milkman said. 'One good thing about it you should keep in mind. In this village nothing ever happens.'

He came down off the porch and stood upon the walk. 'You spoke of the old man,' he said, 'and it was not the old man only. The old lady also left us. The two of them stayed on much beyond their time.'

'You mean I'm here all alone?'

The Milkman had started down the walk, but now he stopped and turned. 'There'll be others coming,' he said. 'There are always others coming.'

What was it Sterling had said about man outrunning his brain capacity? Rand tried to recall the words, but now, in the confusion of the moment, he had forgotten them. But if that should be the case, if Sterling had been right (no matter how he had phrased his thought), might not man need, for a while, a place like this, where nothing ever happened, where the moon was always full and the year was stuck on autumn?

Another thought intruded and Rand swung about, shouting in sudden panic at the Milkman. 'But these others? Will they talk to me? Can I talk with them? Will I know their names?'

The Milkman had reached the gate by now and it appeared that he had not heard.

The moonlight was paler than it had been. The eastern sky was flushed. Another matchless autumn day was about to dawn.

Rand went around the house. He climbed the steps that led up to the porch. He sat down in the rocking chair and began waiting for the others.

Brian Aldiss

FORGOTTEN LIFE

At 49, Clement Winter, distinguished psychoanalyst and Oxford don, is reaching a confusing time of life. Married to Sheila, ex-patient and now hugely successful fantasy writer, the cracks are beginning to show in an outwardly well-ordered and prosperous existence.

For Clement is increasingly perturbed as he pores obsessively over the maze of papers left by his brother Joseph, who has recently died. Joseph, by contrast, led an adventurous if unsettled life, serving with the Forgotten Army in Burma and eventually returning to England after a poignant love affair in Sumatra.

The more he puzzles over the lives of others the more Clement finds his own being called emotionally and professionally into question. Only from its apparent contradictions can life so oddly offer hope and revelation. Ranging from East to West, wartime to the present and the dead to living, *Forgotten Life* shows Brian Aldiss at his most searching and inventive.

'Excited me more than anything else I've read this year.'

Anthony Burgess

C. J. Cherryh

THE PALADIN

Beyond the haunted hills of Mon, lives Shoka, Lord Saukendar, the paragon swordmaster who escaped the corrupt court of Chiyaden for a reclusive life of peace. The veteran master turns away all the hopeful youths who risk their lives to seek his mountain exile and learn his secrets.

But it is the girl named Taizu, disguising herself as a scarred and half-starved urchin, who secures the promise of his tutelage and supasses all the swordsmen he has crossed.

With the Emperor approaching his thirtieth year, Chiyaden's court is still governed by the implacable Lord Ghita while its provinces are overrun by marauding bands of mercenaries and bandits. Only Taizu's passion for justice and revenge can persuade the legendary Lord Saukendar to join her in taking up his sword once more to restore the Throne of Chiyaden to its rightful heir.

'Read *The Paladin* and you'll never settle for another ordinary sword-wielding female.'

Locus

C. J. Cherryh

BROTHERS OF EARTH

Kurt Morgan, last survivor of a star war between humans, crashed on a nameless world and found that it was ruled by the only other human there — a woman of the enemy, the Methi.

Befriended by a young native warrior, Kta, and his family, Kurt becomes one of their household. He learns their customs, their manners, their religion, and falls in love with the beautiful nemet girl, Mim.

But his presence in Nefane has stirred deeply buried feelings and as old racial and family feuds threaten to divide the city and plunge the planet into war, Kurt must reconcile his divided loyalty between his nemet family and his brother of Earth, the Methi.

A wonderfully detailed and complex story of adventure and social imagination.

A Selected List of Fiction Available from Mandarin Books

While every effort is made to keep prices low, it is sometimes necessary to increase prices at short notice. Mandarin Paperbacks reserves the right to show new retail prices on covers which may differ from those previously advertised in the text or elsewhere.

The prices shown below were correct at the time of going to press.

☐	7493 0118 X	**The Wire**	Nik Gowing £3.9■
☐	7493 0136 8	**A Kiss of Fire**	Masako Togawa £3.5■
☐	7493 0144 9	**A Question of Guilt**	Frances Fyfield £2.9■
☐	7493 0112 0	**Night Soldiers**	Alan Furst £3.9■
☐	7493 0034 5	**Questions of Identity**	Bob Cook £2.9■
☐	7493 0076 0	**The Crystal Contract**	Julian Rathbone £3.9■
☐	7493 0110 4	**Ice**	James Follett £2.9■

TV and Film Titles

☐	7493 0101 5	**My Left Foot**	Christy Brown £3.5■
☐	7493 0055 8	**Neighbours I**	Marshall/Kolle £2.9■
☐	7493 0057 4	**Dealers**	Gerald Cole £2.5■
☐	7493 0115 5	**Capital City**	Michael Feeney Callan £3.5■
☐	7493 0132 5	**Great Balls of Fire**	Lewis/Silver £3.■

All these books are available at your bookshop or newsagent, or can be ordered direct from th■ publisher. Just tick the titles you want and fill in the form below.

Mandarin Paperbacks, Cash Sales Department, PO Box 11, Falmouth, Cornwall TR10 9E■

Please send cheque or postal order, no currency, for purchase price quoted and allow t■ following for postage and packing:

UK	55p for the first book, 22p for the second book and 14p for each addition■ book ordered to a maximum charge of £1.75.
BFPO and Eire	55p for the first book, 22p for the second book and 14p for each of the ne■ seven books, thereafter 8p per book.
Overseas Customers	£1.00 for the first book plus 25p per copy for each additional book.

NAME (Block letters) ....

ADDRESS ....

....